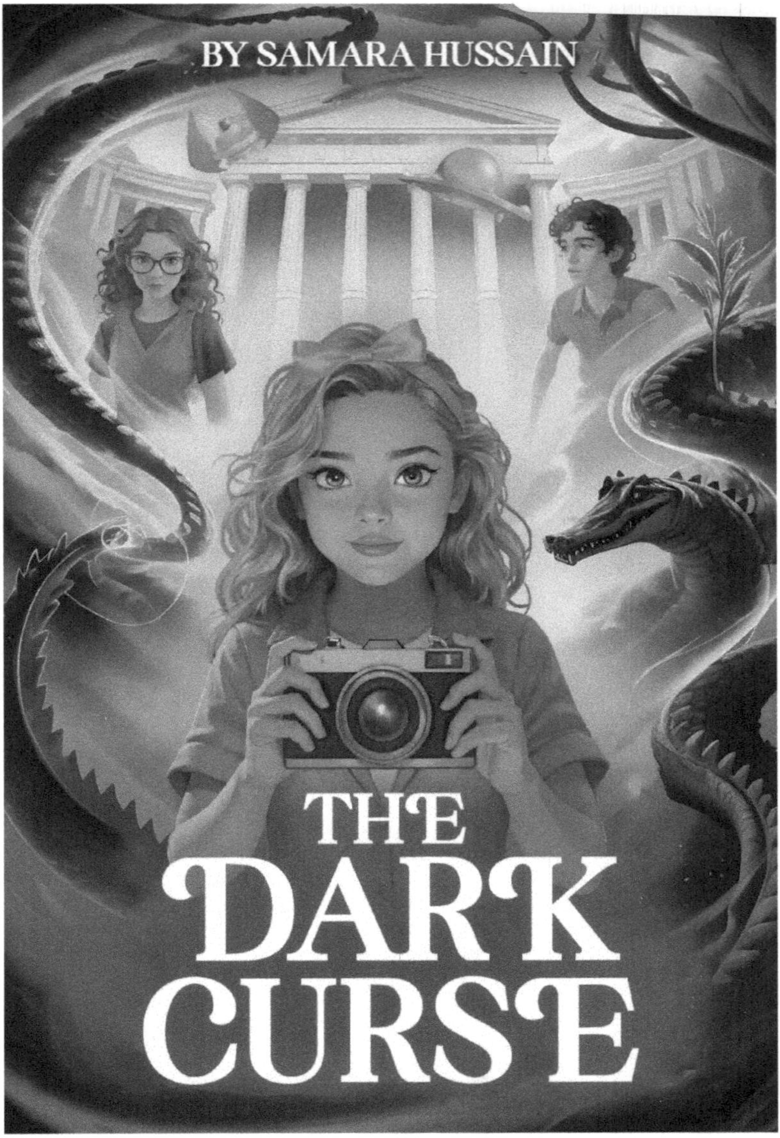

BY SAMARA HUSSAIN

THE DARK CURSE

Dedication

For my amazing Grandmother. Our family feels empty without you.

Prologue

Oh, hey! Didn't see you there. My name is Calliope Canderine, or Calli, as multiple people call me. I am 12 years old and I am in 7th grade at Paideia Middle School. I live with my mom; my dad was a famous astronaut who died mid-air when I was 8 years old. My hobbies are doing photography, practicing archery, and hanging out with my best friends, McKayla (or Kay) Carson and Chris Campbell. This is my story of how my life took a detour while practicing sorcery with my mother.

Table of Contents

Chapter 1 - My Mom Gives Me a Late-Birthday Gift

Chapter 1-My Mom Gives Me a Late-Birthday Gift

"It's the last time, Calli, I promise!" yelled my mother, as she told me the exact same thing she's been telling me for the past month. Calli was my nickname, since Calliope is pretty long. For others, at least. "Why are you making me do this?" I answered her while trying to finish my collage for photography class. She beckoned me downstairs, where a dark basement awaited me and my mom, a... somewhat, magician. The work table was cluttered with potions, books, cameras, and vials of poison from animals. We were currently researching a spell to talk to the dead, something very popular these days. Every single day, my mother would take me downstairs for another dreadful day of witchcraft.

"Why don't you want me to find your father, Calliope!" she asked me. Ouch. My hands clutched onto the railing, as a horrible memory, which haunted me 'till this day, overwhelmed me. I was 8 years old when my father, the famous astronaut Oliver Canderine, went on his last mission to the moon. He had promised me a moon rock, something I had wanted ever since I learned about them. I remembered his funeral. My father, my hero, had died because his spaceship exploded mid-air. He left me all alone with my horrible sorcerer mother. I re-read all the books, and checked all the ingredients. We were ready. My mother started chanting, me trying to keep up with her while reading. The candles flickered, and I dropped Sorcery 101 Part 5 on my feet. "Calliope!" my mother cried, as I fell to the ground. A grey aura filled the big basement. The mist parted, as a man wearing robes was seen. "Daughter," he bellowed at my mom. "Yes, it is me, Hades."

Chapter 2- I Meet My Godly- Grandfather

Chapter 2- I Meet My Godly-Grandfather

"WHAT!" I yelled as I sat up. "He's, like, the Greek god of dead people??? AND MY GRANDFATHER???" I shouted at my mom. If you were in my predicament, you would too. "Calliope, remember the myths and legends your father and I used to tell you when you were younger?" my mother asked soothingly. "I THOUGHT THEY WERE NOT REAL!" "Well, they are, and I want you to meet your grandfather, Hades, the god of the underworld." "Cyrene! I told you NOT to call the dead, and still you didn't listen!" Hades, my supposed grandfather, said.

"Father, I am calling Oliver for Calliope! My daughter!" My mom's eyes brimmed with tears. "Alright, backup! Who are you, and why are you yelling at my mom!" I said. I suddenly felt a wave of protection over my mother. "Stay out of this, girl." He told me. Anger surged through me while Hades yelled at my mother, ending with something I never thought would happen. "CYRENE CANDERINE! You shall be cursed by Hades, the god of the underworld, and you shall never be able to cast another spell, EVER!" A light came from Hades' hand and went through my mother. "NO!" both my mom and I screamed, as a blinding light filled the air.

Chapter 3- I Create a Horrible Plan

Chapter 3- I Create a Horrible Plan

I woke up in my basement, with my mother next to me. Was this a dream? Did my mother really get her powers revoked? I asked myself while in an attempt to sit up. "Mom!" I yelled, trying to wake her up. Her eyes fluttered open, revealing her dark-grey eyes. I immediately held her head to my chest, hugging her. Tears flowed down my cheeks while accepting my new life. My mother no longer had her sorcery, something I resented since FOREVER. She pushed away, and surprisingly, her eyes weren't red or wet. "Well, that was quite a day. I'll see you at dinner," she said, kissing me on my forehead. She bounded up the staircase to the bright world above. I slowly got up and trudged up the stairs, not sure what had just happened. I went upstairs to my room, which *was filled with pictures from the past, something I will soon miss very much. I took a book, one I haven't read since the night before the space launch. It was the mythology book I had gotten from Greece. I went there with my mom and dad when I was 5. It was probably my favorite trip. I skimmed through until I found Hades. It gave me all sorts of facts, but it never said anything about the children of the gods. As I looked at the walls of my bedroom, a horribly splendid idea came to my mind. I would find the Underworld and make Hades, AKA Grandpa, take back the curse he gave my mom.*

Chapter 4- I Meet the Chocolate-Eyed Boy

Chapter 4- I Meet the Chocolate-Eyed Boy

I pulled my blanket over my head as my alarm rang. I had just woken up from an eerie nightmare. Beads of sweat fell on my face as I walked to my bathroom and got dressed. Breakfast was, as usual, pancakes and blueberries. I scarfed them down as quickly as I could. My mother and I started talking about school, but I could sense some sadness in her voice. She had told me the night before that she had dedicated her entire life to magic and sorcery, just to get to know her father more. But all her life's work was simply gone. Before my bus came, I went down to the basement. There were still a little bit of supplies here and there, books were still on the shelves, but otherwise, our former workroom was empty.

BEEP BEEP. That was my cue to run upstairs. I ran to my bus and I saw somebody. I never saw him on the bus before, so I figured he was new. This new kid was a couple of inches taller than me; he looked around 5'6". He, honestly, looked a bit lost. Everyone was whispering and stealing glances at this new kid. As I walked down the aisle, I tripped on somebody's foot. Carissa. I have always fought with her. She always bullies me for no reason. I hate her. I dropped my lunch kit, and all its contents fell out. I was on my knees when the new kid crouched and started helping me clean up. He had black curly hair and sandy skin. Up close, his dark chocolate- colored eyes were the most beautiful eyes I have ever seen.

"Hi, my name is Chris. Chris Campbell," he said. My mind just stopped functioning. I could hear alarms ringing in my ear, telling me to say something!!!! "Hey! My name is Calliope Canderine. Thanks for helping with my things." "You're welcome." I invited him to my seat and we talked a little bit. The bus finally arrived at my school, Paideia Middle School, where I was in the 7th grade. I learnt that Chris was also in 7th grade, which made me a tad bit excited. We also had the same homeroom teacher, Mrs. Kasweda. I was surprised to know that, A, I was assigned as his 'Tour Guide' and B, he also had a Photography with me! During lunch, I invited him to my table, after giving him the warning that we were all nerds, bookworms, and geeks. He didn't seem to mind. Actually, he got along with a lot of my friends, practically everyone.

My neighbor, BFF, and practical sister, McKayla Carson, came to me, and we both walked to science together. She knew all about my mother and her magic, so I told her about the night before, and my horrendous plan. "Cool," she said, smiling, " Count me in!" This was one of the many reasons that I was still friends with her. We may have had our rough patches, but she always calmed me down when I was mad, and she was always, ALWAYS positive. I wondered if she had the superpower of patience. Mr. Silva, our science teacher, gave us a pop quiz. I got a 100 on it; it was pretty easy for me. I saw Kay struggling with the problems. Since we sat next to each other, I would give her the answers, just so that I could pay her back for all she does for me. Right after, it was time for my favorite class, Photography with Ms. Arnyam!

I sat next to Chris, who got there earlier than me, and introduced him to Ms. Arnyam. "It was nice meeting you, Chris, and I can see *that you have already met Calli," she told him. While finishing our collages (which Chris could do perfectly), I kept on staring at Chris. I mean, if you've seen him, you would too. But then, he caught me staring, so I quickly looked away, my cheeks coloring. After class, we were dismissed, and Chris asked me if he could talk to me privately. I blushed while walking with him. "Do you believe in the Greek Gods?" he asked me tentatively. I exhaled and started laughing. "What? Are you making fun of me?" he asked, looking worried. He looked cute when he was worried. "No, sorry," I told him, stifling my giggles. Then, I proceeded to tell him about my mom and Hades.*

🛏 Chapter 5-I Get my Phone Taken

Chapter 5- I Get My Phone Taken

I was lying on my bed, deep in thought about what Chris had told me earlier, when there was a knock on my door. I opened my door, just to find my mother outside. "Hey, Calli. McKayla sent you something on your phone," she said, "Something urgent." I immediately snatched my magenta (that's my favorite color) phone and ran to my bed. "Remember, once you are done, I want your phone downstairs." "Yes, Ma'am," I told her while reading Kay's message. Hey. I did some research on the Underworld and Hades, and this was the best reference. & no, it is not Wikipedia. Love, Kay♡

In case you didn't know, I hate Wikipedia. I clicked on the link. It took me to a website. I skimmed through the paragraphs. I read things about Furies (or the Erninyes), the River Styx, and other places in the Underworld. It felt like HOURS, and I was not done when my mom knocked again. Supposedly, it was too late, so I walked downstairs, put my phone up, and went to my room. When I went to bed, I replayed what had happened at school with Chris.

Chapter 6 - Chris Reveals His Secrets

Chapter 6- Chris Reveals His Secrets

We were next to our photography class when Chris broke his news to me. "My grandmother is a Greek goddess, Aphrodite," he told me. He explained his entire heritage in a span of 15-20 minutes. His family line was ancient, and they came from Ithaca, Greece. They fought in the Trojan War and then moved to Rome afterwards. His dad was a son of Aphrodite. He never knew his mom, though. She was Greek, not the ancient kind, but she died while on a plane. All I could think, when he talked about his mom, was my dad. He also died in the air, on his spacecraft. He also had a 21-year-old sister who lived in New York. She moved out when Chris was 2. For some random reason, I trusted him enough to tell him about my stupid, dumb idea. Chris didn't hesitate for a second. He was ready to join. "How did you find out about this stuff?" I asked him. "My dad always told me the stories of ancient Greece and its gods," he replied anxiously. "You believe me?" he asked. "Of course! I legitimately just saw my godly grandparent yesterday! Also, you are now my friend, and I, for one, am not a person who doesn't trust a friend," I assured him, as we walked towards our bus. We had exchanged phone numbers on the bus to keep in touch with each other, in case something mythological happened to any of our families. His phone case was the color green; he said that, in the pictures, his mom's eyes were that color. (That is very sweet of him, if you ask me.)

Chapter 7 - My Friend Get Possessed By Holmes

Chapter 7- My Friend Gets Possessed by Holmes

GURL! You forgot about the playdate! HOW DARE YOU! 😠😠😠- Kay Gosh, if she were my mom, I would be grounded every day, because I am kind of forgetful... ANYWAYS, I had also forgotten to ask my mom about it, with Hades declaring himself as my divine grandfather, and whatnot. As I crept downstairs, thinking of ways to convince my mom, I saw Kay's bag on the shoe rack. Of course. I cannot spend ONE DAY without some surprise. Oh joy. "Calli!" my mom called, "McKayla's here!" Once I arrived at the sitting room, she added, "And yes, you may go to your friend's playdate and sleepover." Booyah! I quickly thanked my mom, packed my bag, and walked to McKayla's house. "Hi, Calli!" said her mom as we entered. If I had to pick someone else to be my mom, it would be Mrs. Carson. She was the absolute sweetest person in the world! She was also one of my mom's friends since high school, so Kay and I had practically grown up together. That's also why she was my BFF; she was my sister! When we reached her house, breakfast was on the table. Chocolate chip muffins, dragon fruit, with a chocolate milkshake. Delicious. As usual, I stuffed the food down my throat like the starving animal I am. After that, Kay and I ran upstairs to her bedroom.

"Okay, so, here's the deal," Kay started, as she ripped the bedsheet covering her wall. Oh. My. God. That woman had done literal research on Hades and the Underworld, even more than me. That kind of concerned me. There were points, and strings connected references and clues. "Girl," I told her," You are not Sherlock Holmes! What is all of this for!" I know that sounds ungrateful, but I was really shocked. She didn't need to do all that. "For you, you ding-dong. I know how much your mother means to you, and I don't care if you deny it. Also, I am your sister, okay? And sisters do these kinds of things for each other. And also," she kept on saying," you would do the same for me."

Gosh, thank goodness this side of her doesn't come out this often. The irrational, bestie side of her. "But you didn't have to do that! I could have figured it all out on my own!" I yelled at her. "Oh, yeah?!" she yelled back. "Then tell me, how and what would you have figured out by yourself, hmm?!" I lowered my head, ashamed. She had done so much, but I screamed at her, telling her I didn't need her help. And I did need her help, and I was the one who told her about Hades and let her research so much. Her face was red, while mine was burning. Tears fell down my face, and Kay came over and hugged me. She did that whenever I cried. I was, once more, overwhelmed by a flashback. I was back at my dad's funeral, and I was sobbing horribly. I'm sorry, but when I feel and experience these huge

emotions, I break down, crying. And, also, that was rational. Anyways, McKayla comes over, and hugs me close. "Calm down, Calli," she whispers, "It'll be alright." Nobody really knows about this side of me, except my mom, my dad, and Kay. "It's alright," Kay from the present whispered, "Sorry for crashing out on you, though." Between sniffles, I accepted her apology, and McKayla brought me a box of tissues. "Where do you get all those tears from?" she asks me with a smirk. I guess we're back to normal, I thought distantly. "Alright, back to business," Kay said, showing me her Holmes-esque wall. "Kay," I tentatively say. She raises her eyebrow. "You know that new kid, Chris, right?" She nodded.

"So, like, how do I explain it... But, like, I think we should ask him for help with this." "Why?" "Because..." "Because?" she prompts. "Because he is also a grandchild of a Greek god."

Chapter 8– Kay Decides to Yell at Me

Chapter 8- Kay Decides to Yell at Me.

Again, "WHAT???" she yells," and you just FORGOT to mention this!!??" "Gosh," I say," calm down, bro, you are scaring me with the yelling voice. With my mom having her magic revoked, and me finding out Hades is my divine gramps, I didn't get any time, I promise!" "Besides," I added," I already am so forgetful. You know that Kay!" "Fine, tell me who he is related to," she says grudgingly. I told her what Chris told me during school the other day. After I'm done, McKayla's mouth dangles open. "I am kinda jealous of you guys, now," she says.

"My parents are completely normal, while you guys get the God of the Underworld and the Goddess of Love as your grandparents." "If you were going through what I am, then you wouldn't want that," I grumble under my breath. "What?" "Nothing." "So, you have his phone number?" I nod. "Then, call him!" she told me. I shrugged and pulled out my phone to call him. We convinced him to come over to Kay's house, after asking permission, of course, and in a few minutes, he was at the front door. "Thanks for inviting me to do homework, guys," Chris says while going upstairs. P.S. We didn't have any homework, thankfully. He couldn't be any more suspicious with his sarcastic voice...

Once we entered Kay's room, McKayla and I took turns telling our plan. We also tell him that Kay knows his heritage and that she was in our weird little search group for Hades. "Okay," I say, "here's the plan. We look at the research McKayla had done on Hades and the possible locations for the Underworld." As we look at the Post-it notes on her wall, we all conclude. "So, the Underworld is somewhere near Houston, Texas?" I ask, and the others shrug. Houston was about an hour away from our town, Cypress. Cypress was part of the Greater Houston area, so you might think I technically lived in Houston. Cypress is not really in Houston, though. (I'll stop; you don't want me to rant about my geological location.) Also, I had horrible memories of Houston.

"Calli?" Kay asked, "You good?" Of course, it was my BFF who realized what I was thinking. Houston was where I last saw my dad. Suddenly, I was pulled into a flashback, and I fainted. The last thing I heard was Kay's scream.

Chapter 9 - Houston, We Have a Problem

Chapter 9- Houston, We Have a Problem

"My Muse," said a voice which I very much recognized. My dad had said that to me before getting ready to go into his spacecraft. He called me his 'Muse', in honor of my namesake, the Greek Muse of Poetry. I was crying (obviously). For some reason, I felt like I would never see him again. I was right, but I didn't know at the time. My dad wiped a tear from my cheek, lifted me into his arms, and hugged me hard. I was full-on sobbing by then, wiping my tears on his shoulder. "Calli, listen," he told me, " You still want that moonrock?" I nodded.

"Well," he continued, "You will get your moonrock, I promise." He put me down and hugged my mom, who was starting to get teary-eyed. He whispered something in her

ear, something I didn't hear or pay attention to. Eventually, I would find out what my dad was talking about, but I had no idea what it was back then. She nodded, and she lifted me up. My mom, back then, was normal, loving, and not into witchcraft. Yet. We waved goodbye, and my amazing father turned right. We would never see him again. During atmospheric entry, a week later, the spacecraft exploded mid-air, taking my dad with it, never to be seen again. My ears rang with pathetic phrases full of fake empathy: "Sorry," "He was very brave,"

"Poor you, losing your father so early in life." Whenever I would hear somebody losing someone, I made sure I would never say the words those pitiful people told me. We got a medal in his honor, which I ABSOLUTELY hated. "Oh, sorry that your dad died during one of *our missions. Here, this medal is for you!" was quite literally what they meant when they delivered this to our house. In my darkest moments, I heard voices telling me. Telling me that they're sorry for my loss and all that trash. The funeral was also when Kay and I became better friends than we were before. Ever since then, I HATED Houston, TX.* With my luck, to save my mother's life's work, I had to go back there and face my trauma. Oh, joy.

Chapter 10 - We Make Connections with my Flashbacks

Chapter 10- We Make Connections with My Flashbacks

"CALLI!!" I opened my eyes and saw Kay's face, her browline, maroon- colored glasses, her almond-shaped, hazel eyes brimmed with tears, her button nose, and her curled, luxurious, caramel hair. "I'm alive, don't worry," I say weakly. Kay tackled me in a hug, and wept into my shoulder. Honestly, I was surprised. After the little argument we got into earlier, I expected her not to be this emotional. She pulled away and punched my arm very hard. "IF YOU DO THAT ONE. MORE. TIME, I WILL MURDER YOU!!!" she yells at me.

I just laughed, apologizing to both of them. "Calliope, what happened, though?" Chris asked. He had his cute, worrying face on. Adorable. I soon felt guilty that I forgot about him. I told both of them about my flashbacks. "So," Chris says, "how long have you been having flashbacks?" I tried to remember the 1st time I had a flashback. "I think it started when I was in 4th grade," I told them. Kay put on her "thinking face". It's when she scrunches her eyebrows and squints her eyes. "So," Kay says, "let's get back on track, shall we?" After what felt like forever, I broke the silence.

"Did anyone come up with ideas of where the entrance to the Underworld could be?" I glanced at Chris, who was deep in thought. "Calli, McKayla," he finally says, "Am I the only one who thinks that Calli's flashbacks are connected to our mission?" Oh. I hadn't thought of that. "So what you are saying," Kay says, " is that the entrance to the Underworld is near Space Center Houston?" Chris nodded. I considered it. "That could make sense," I said.

"Wait," I continued, "remember that site you sent me, Kay?" She nods. "I think it said something about Hades being able to control darkness." Then, Chris said," And, your flashbacks were nothing if they weren't dark, in a figurative way." "So," Kay asked uncertainly, "you guys are saying that Hades may be giving Calli hints and controlling her flashbacks. And if he is, then why? Didn't he revoke your mom's power, never to be used again?" She had a point. "I am not sure," I admit, " But I am willing to take that chance." Kay looked at me warily and said, "You are absolutely bonkers." I grin. Whenever she declares that I am crazy, it mostly means that she agreed with whatever I said. Which was great. "Now," I say, "We need to convince our parents to let us go to Houston." "What if we ask one of our teachers?" Chris asked. "Or seek divine help?" I didn't consider that either. If *my mom can summon someone as powerful as Hades, then we can summon someone a deity too. A minor, weaker one, I guessed. "What if I go to my basement, where my mom worked on her magic, and scavenge for something that can conjure a Greek god?" Kay shrugged, while Chris gave me a thumbs-up. Perfect. "McKayla!" Mrs. Carson called, "Chris's dad is here to pick him up!" I had completely forgotten, again, that Chris wasn't here for our sleepover. "Well," he says, "I guess I have to go now." We said our goodbyes, but just as he was about to go downstairs, I intervened. "Hey, Chris?" He looked towards me with his gorgeous eyes. "Thanks." He smiled (which made my stomach go berserk), gave me a thumbs-up, and went to the front door. "Ooooh!" Kay said, "Looks like someone has a CRUSH!" "SHUT UP!" I slapped her arm and chased her back to her room.*

We kept on talking about ways that we could convince our parents to let us go to Houston, when her mom told us to turn off the lights. "Calli," Kay whispered. I looked at her. "Be real with me right now. Are you scared?" "Honestly, Kay?" I tell her, "A little bit." She throws her cat Squishmallo, which I gave her for her birthday. She had named it Clio, after the Greek Muse of History, and the sister of my namesake, Calliope. Now that I think of it, maybe my name was a hint about my heritage. Anyways, whenever I was sad, Kay would pass me Clio, and she would let me hold it for a while. "Thanks," I mumbled. "Hey," Kay said, " Don't be so glum! We'll figure it out!"

I laughed without humor and slowly went to sleep. I guess it wasn't enough that I got tormented in the daytime. Of course not! I also NEED to have nightmares!

Chapter 11– I Get Bit in Greece

Chapter 11- I Get Bit in Greece

My nightmares started like this: I was 5 years old again, and I was back in Greece. That trip was probably my favorite trip in my entire life, and it was with my dad, which made it infinitely better. Here's a little back story: My dad, for his research on space rocks, would go to different places to find the rocks. Me and my mom would often tag along. I loved to help Dad with his work. I learned a whole bunch of things about space because of him. Anyways, back to my horrid nightmare. We were in Ithaca, Greece, the home of the legendary king Odysseus. Me My dad, my mom were walking on the Gidaki beach, known for its stunning walks. The sun was setting.

Oh, god. I remembered exactly what happened on that day. There had been an alligator attack on Gidaki beach, right when I was there with my parents. The alligator came out of nowhere and grabbed onto my little leg, as if there weren't any more around. I cried in terror, tears running down my face. To be honest, I still am scared of reptiles since that incident. If not for my dad, I would've gotten my leg chopped off. Suddenly, my dream took a wrong turn. This time, nobody helped me; I was all alone. My mind was still of a 5-year-old, so I kept on yelling, not trying to defend myself. Finally, the alligator let go and went away. Blood gushed from my leg, turning my pastel blue tights the color purple. Not a good sign. I tried to stand up, but the pain was too much.

"Help," I croaked weakly, but nobody was there to hear my cries. Soon, the pain was unbearable. I knew that I was going to end up severely injured, or even amputated.

Chapter 12– I Scare the Hades Out of Everyone

Chapter 12- I Scare the Hades Out of Everyone

"CALLI! WAKE UP!" I woke up with sweat forming on my forehead. "Gosh, Kay, what happened?" I asked. It was about 4 AM, and I was pretty sure Kay didn't wake up this early. "You were sobbing, bro! You were yelling, calling for your dad, so I was worried." Of course, she was. "Sorry, Kay. I was having a nightmare." Kay's eyes widened with concern. "What did you see?" she asked me. I told her about my dream. "Ouch," she said, finally. "And you still have the scar?" I nodded, rolling up my right pant leg to show her.

Even after 7 years, the bite was red, but something about it seemed... different. It was glowing dimly, or something. "Calli?" McKayla asked, "Does your wound glow like that all the time?" I shook my head, clearly mystified. Kay ran out of her door. "Kay!" I called out, getting up, but my knees buckled. I groaned in pain. Kay came back with her mom. "Calliope," she asked softly, "Are you okay?" At this point, I was crying, in both embarrassment and pain. I didn't know Kay would be THAT concerned; that she would call her mom. I slightly shrugged, my body aching. "I should call your mom," said Mrs. Carson. "I'm fine," I protested, but deep down, I knew I wasn't.

Following the attack, I had gotten 6 months of therapy, and my knees hadn't given away since then. Of course, Mrs. Carson knew about it. "Calli?" said my mom's voice on the phone, full of concern. I sobbed. I knew that this would worry my mom even more, but I couldn't control it. "I'll be right there," said my mom, hanging up. Both Kay and her mom looked anxious. They probably haven't seen me like this before, and I am a somewhat healthy person, you know? My mother, dear, rushed into the room, her grey eyes tight with anxiety. I knew that feeling. She was going to break down if I didn't pull myself together. I got up, groaning in pain. "I'm fine, Mom." Now that I look back, I was really worried about my mom, who was worried for me. I know y'all remember how I would hate my mom, but since the thing with Hades, she was warming up to me. "Calli, does it hurt a lot?" asked Kay, concerned. I nodded. I was not helping the mood. At. All. My mom tried to pick me up, to take me to the hospital. At this point, Kay was crying. She hated injuries and gore, especially if they were on me. Mom took me to our car, Kay trailing behind. "Kay, dear," said my mom, "You should go." After a lot of protesting from McKayla, she sat next to me in our purple Toyota Prius. I was sweating a lot, and I was still in my space pajamas, with a serious case of bed hair. I didn't care about those things, though. The only thing that mattered was the pain in my shin.

Upon arrival, I was put in a wheelchair and taken to urgent care. People came and went, but my mother and Kay were by my side the entire time. The doctor, after examining my foot, deduced that I had gotten an infection that was never cured. Even though she said that my bite had never been treated, my mom and I could swear it was healed. But the doctor didn't listen. She prescribed some medicine, which we could get from our local Walgreens, and sent us on our way. I could walk a little, by then, but not without support. "Thanks," I told Kay once we dropped her at her house. She just shrugged and walked back. My mom looked at the mirror and raised an eyebrow. "What happened, Calliope?"

She knew what was wrong. She would know about my plan, and order me NOT to do it. I shook my head. This time, my mom looked back and looked me in the eye. "Calli," she said calmly, "I know when something is wrong with you. It is seen clearly in your stormy, grey eyes." "It is nothing, Mom," I said, which caused her to raise her eyebrows once more. "But," she continued, "You will tell me if there is, right?" I nodded and raised my hand in a mock salute.

Once we reached home, I tried going upstairs without my mom's help, which made Hercules' 12 labors look easy. I trudged into my bedroom, but it was already 6 am, so sleep didn't come to me. Instead of sleeping, I picked up my phone. Knock Knock. It was my mom. I called her inside.

"Calli," she said, her voice full of tenderness, "Your contemplating face is on." "I don't have a 'contemplating face', Mom," I told her. "Yes, you do, just like your dad." I was dumbfounded. "What?" I never realized the fact that my dad had a 'contemplating face'. I guess, since I haven't seen him since I was 8, I forgot about it, but still, I was surprised. I stared at the photo of my family on my wall, next to my clock. My dad's bright smile, his brown retro square glasses, his pitch-black eyes (which did not match his personality), his pastel blue dress shirt, his curly, blonde hair. My mom standing next to him, wearing her blue gown, her dark, wavy hair, her dark grey eyes, her pink lips. Me standing in front of them, my stormy grey eyes, my dirty blonde hair, curled at the ends, wearing an azure blue dress (my favorite when I was younger) and a tiara. It was a picture from my 8th birthday, the last I shared with my dad. I started crying, seeing that picture. Why does my luck suck so much! Why can't I have a normal life, with a normal mom, a living dad, and a non-godly grandfather. My only wish was to have my life back to normal. My mom came closer, and gave me a hug. She understood how I felt. After a long time, I realized that my mom wasn't as bad as I thought. She pecked my forehead. "Calli, you should rest," she told me. I nodded. "Without your phone," she added, snatching it from my hand. I groaned. Even though I was hurt, I still got my phone taken away. Great.

CHAPTER 13- KAY'S MARVELOUS PLAN

Chapter 13- Kay's Marvelous Plan (Which She Comes Up Because of Me, Obviously)

Later that day, McKayla came over to visit me with her 'homework' (psst, it was research from the day before; don't tell anyone). I was stuck in my room, and I wasn't allowed to go out. Ugh. Moms and their restrictions. Anyways, we left the door slightly ajar to avoid suspicion, and we got back to work. For some reason, Kay didn't mention what happened in the early morning. Weird. But I don't blame her, though. I still cannot think about that without my foot hurting. "Alright," she started, "We know where the Underworld is, but a couple of questions remain. For example, how we can get to Space Center Houston is currently a mystery." "Did you binge-watch Sherlock Holmes recently?" I asked her. "Girl, shut up and focus," she answered with a smirk. Thank god. My best friend hasn't been possessed by some detective. Suddenly, an idea popped into my head. "So, since the Underworld should be underneath us, right?" I asked her. She nodded. "Why don't we figure out the lowest level or door there?" "Are we including restricted areas?" she asked. Never mind what I said earlier. She HAD been possessed by some detective. "We should," I answered. "We can use my family line, as in my famous astronaut father, to get into those places."

"Where is this going, Calli?" she asked. "Think about it," I told her, "How many times have people given me pitiful looks when they found out about my dad dying? We could use that to our advantage, right?" She nodded, clearly warming up to the idea. "So, to conclude, we have to go to Space Center Houston, find the lowest point, ignore the restrictions, use the pity people give you as our 'access', and find Hades to get your mom's powers back, is that it?" Kay asked. I nodded. "But, we need to know HOW to get there." She continued, "All this work will be for nothing if we cannot find a way to go there." Suddenly, her face brightened up. Uh, oh. "Kay," I asked, cautiously, "What are you thinking?" "You know how beautiful the inside of Space Center Houston is, right?"

I nodded. "What if we could ask Ms. Arnyam if we could go on a field trip there!" "God, Kay, that is an AMAZING IDEA!" For ya'll who didn't know, McKayla is also in Photography Class, even though she is only there because of me and the teacher. You also may have noticed that we weren't in the same class period. She has theater when I have Photography. So, all we had to do was to tell Ms. Arnyam whenever we got to school.

Chapter 14- I Think Something's Wrong

Chapter 14- I Think Something's Wrong...

The next day was Monday, so we had school. The night before, Kay and I had filled up Chris on our plan, which he agreed was genius, lifting Kay's spirits. I was able to walk again by then (yay!). My foot still hurt, though, so I was excused from athletics (bigger yay!). Before leaving, though, I went down to the basement to see what I could scavenge. There were some books and vials here and there, but it still felt really bare. I looked around for something that could help us summon a deity when something caught my eye.

It was the Sorcery 101 Part 5 book I was holding when Hades appeared. There MUST be some spell that could summon a god, right? Before I could open it, my bus arrived. I stuffed the book in my pack, and went towards my bus, saying goodbye to my mom. "Oh, sweetie," said an annoying voice once I entered the bus. It was Carissa. Ugh, I hated her. "I saw you at the hospital the other day with your mommy holding your hand," she said. My face burned while her friends snickered. "Calli! Over here," said Chris, waving at me from the 6th row. Saved by the Chris, I thought, walking towards him. "So, how's your foot?" he asked. I shrugged. "Oh, yeah," I said, remembering the book in my bag, "I found something."

His eyes widened when I pulled out the Sorcery 101 Part 5 book. "I had this in my hand when Hades appeared," I told him. "Wow, so, this could help us in the summoning?" I nodded. Right then, our bus arrived at Paideia Middle School. As we walked to class, I bumped into somebody. "CALLI!"   It was Kay. She was coming from the library, but something felt off. God, I just realized. The cast list for theater was going to be posted up today, and she really wanted to be the main role. "You good, bro?" She shook her head. I hadn't seen her this sad before. "I got picked as an ensemble," she said in a small voice.

"WHAT!?"   In case you haven't seen Kay act before, she was a NATURAL! She should've won billions of acting awards by now. "And Carissa and her group were teasing me." I clenched my fists, shaking with anger. It was one thing to bully me all the time, but my BFF was off limits.   I ran off to find that little brat, ignoring Kay and Chris protesting. There she was, ordering her dumb minions around, applying make-up. She was laughing in her annoying way. "Carissa," I said, my voice dangerously calm. Now that I think back, I actually was being led by my rage. Nobody, absolutely nobody teases McKayla. "Ugh, here is the baby whose mommy was holding her hand in the hospital," she said, making all her friends laugh.

Then, all Hades broke loose. My instincts told me to face my palm towards Carissa. Suddenly, a black light came from my palm and hit her mirror, disintegrating the glass. Carissa and her gang ran away, running. My brain told me to stop, but I didn't want to. Stupid Carissa had been rude to me since FOREVER.

And I wanted to take revenge on her.

"CALLI!" yelled a voice behind me.

It was Kay, running with Chris behind her.

I turned around, facing them. McKayla had fear in her eyes, but that wasn't because of

Carissa. It was because of me. The adrenaline washed away, and I was scared of myself, too.

How did I do that? Was that a trick? No, it wasn't. The mirror in Carissa's hand had turned to dust.

I fell to my knees in horror. What was this new power?

"Calli!" Kay yelled, grabbing my shoulders. "Are you alright? What happened to Carissa and her friends? How did-"

"I don't know," I said quietly, "I don't know, Kay." "Clearly," said Chris, "It was some Hades power, you know? That dark light looked like shadows."

I was astounded. "You guys think I'm in trouble?" I asked them. Soon, a teacher came up behind me. It was Ms. Arnyam, our photography teacher. "Kids," she said quietly, "What happened here?" We just awkwardly glanced at each other, not knowing what to say.

I think Ms. A realized something wasn't right. She closed her eyes, and suddenly, the dust was all gone! It was as if nothing had happened! "Ms. A-"

"Say nothing and follow me," she said, cutting me off.

She ushers us into her room, currently unoccupied.

"Calliope," she said calmly, "Do you know what you did?"

I was scared. I thought Ms. Arnyam would get mad at me. I shrugged, not knowing what to do. She just nodded. "And do you know what I just did?" This time, Chris spoke up. "I'm guessing you somehow erased the event from everyone's memory, except ours, right?" She nodded once more. "What," I said, "So, our photography teacher can alter memories?" "Yes," Ms. A answered calmly. "And I know both of you guys' heritages," she added. "Calli is the granddaughter of Hades, while Chris is the grandson of Aphrodite."

All three of our jaws dropped. "H-how did-" "I know because I am like you guys," she said. "My grandmother is Lethe, the goddess of forgetfulness and oblivion, while my mother is Hecate, goddess of magic, crossroads, and the veil that keeps the mortal realm away from the magical realm." "The whaaaa?" I asked, my mind not comprehending anything. "The veil, also known as the Fog, makes sure that mortals cannot see abnormal events, like what you did with the mirror, Calli."

I was surprised. But I was also relieved. If Ms. Arnyam could have a life just like mine, that meant my life didn't suck as much!

I locked eyes with Kay, who was also speechless. She may have been astonished, but her eyes said otherwise.

Tell her about our plan, it seemed to tell me.

If my bestie was asking me to tell Ms. A about our plan, even though we might get in big trouble, I would. I started talking to Ms. Arnyam about what happened to my mom, and our plan to fix everything. While I talked, I realized small details about her appearance. For example, her silky hair was actually a really dark shade of brown, not black, and her eyes were a little lighter than dark grey; not exactly black, but not dark grey like mine either. This time, it was her turn to be surprised. "Wow, so you 3 came up with this on your own?" We nodded. "Alright. Save me a spot, then!" We three looked at each other. We expected some protesting and lectures not to go along with our plan, not her just saying yes immediately. "So, you will plan a trip to Space Center Houston." "I actually have a better idea," she said, a smile coming on her face. Just then, the tardy bell rang, signifying that we only had 3 minutes to get to class. "You guys should go now," Ms. A said. We nodded, and we quickly went to our homeroom classes. Kay went to Mr. Cummings' Language Arts class, while Chris and I went to Mrs. Kasweda's class.

Chapter 15- To Calli, Kay, and Chris

Chapter 15- To Calli, Kay, and Chris.

Love Ms. A During Photography class, Ms. Arnyam informed Chris and I that she has asked permission for us to stay behind to finish our "project". She told Kay's mom, too. So, there we were after school, sitting around Ms. A's desk. My eyes were on her desk, which was covered with a lot of donut- themed items. I guess she really liked donuts. But, my ears were on Ms. Arnyam who was telling us an even better idea. "What if," she started, "I tell your parents that you 3 have been doing so well, that I want to take you guys to Space Center Houston to enhance your photography even more!" She was good.

"Ms. A," I said, "That is BRILLIANT! That way, you can be part of our little group to find Hades!" Her face fell. Oh, no. "I can take you guys to Houston, but I cannot take you any further. This is clearly your quest; not mine to undertake." "But-" "No buts, no ifs, Calli," she told me. "If you want to help your mom get her magic back, which I completely agree with, being a daughter of the goddess of magic, you will have to do it yourself." I must've looked really disappointed because Kay said, "Hey, you aren't alone. You've got your best friends, girly. You ain't alone in this." Chris nodded, giving me a thumbs up. "Let us get back to business, then," I said, determined to not let them see me vulnerable. "When are we planning to go, Ms. A?" I asked her.

"2 things," she said. "First of all, now that we are partners in crime, you can call me Raya, not Ms. A. Plus, we're technically not at school. I'm not your teacher, I am your friend, your helper. Secondly," she continued, "I asked if this Saturday would be alright, and they said yes." I loved Ms. A, sorry, Raya in our group. She would, obviously, be the brains of our operation. "Thanks, Ms. A- I mean Raya," I sincerely said, giving her a hug. She had always been my favorite teacher, but she had gotten to a whole new level for favorite. She was now the BEST teacher in the world. I challenge you to tell me if you have had better teachers. ANYWAYS, the hug startled her, but she slowly melted into it. "I knew you were something different, Calli," she told me, stroking my hair.

I blushed right to the roots of my dirty blonde hair. Once I pulled away, I called Mom to come pick us up. Mom kept on staring at us while driving home, but she didn't notice anything fishy, thankfully.

Chapter 16- The Boring Things

Chapter 16- The Boring Things

You Might Want to Know The next few days went like this: I would meet Chris in the mornings to talk about ourselves (while stealing glances of him and staring in his dark chocolate eyes); I would tolerate Carissa during math (while trying not to disintegrate anything); My ELAR teacher would give me new books to read (which I wouldn't even touch); I would eat lunch with Kay, Chris, and all my nerdy/geek friends (who were all acting weirdly); I would give Kay the answers in science (without Mr. Silva noticing); Chris and I would talk about 'tutoring' with Ms. Arnyam; Kay would ride home with us on the bus (her parents had some important meeting, so she would stay over at my house [yay!]); Then, we would talk strategy at night. Then, on the bus,

Chris and I would talk more about each other (One time, he showed me his phone's wallpaper, which had a picture of him and his mom. He looked adorable...) That was how our weekdays went, until Saturday arrived. That was when we would see if our planning would come through.

Chapter 17- Before the Trip

Chapter 17- Before the Trip

I woke up early that day because of my anxiety. I crept out of my room, careful not to wake up Kay. Last night, she had broken down, crying. She hated doing anything dangerous, and this quest was nothing if not dangerous. I asked her if she didn't want to come along, but she got her serious face on and said, "I may be scared, but I won't back down now, not when you need me." I gave her a hug, which took her by surprise. She quickly pulled away and got back to nerding out about her favorite book. I went downstairs to the kitchen and found my mother already awake. She turned around and smiled at me. "You're up early," she said, "Did you need anything?"

I shook my head. "I was wondering what is for breakfast." That wasn't really what I came down for, but if I told my mother that I was anxious about something, she would force me to tell her what the 'something' was. Instead of interrogating, she laughed gently. "Of course you were. I decided to make something new for you guys today." My face must have shown absolute glee because my mom laughed again and told me to go upstairs. When I went back, McKayla was awake. "'Morning, sleepyhead," I teased. She didn't answer. She was scrolling through her phone. "What is so important on there, Kay?" I asked her, sitting criss-crossed next to her. She turned her phone screen towards me. My jaw dropped.

Her screen showed a news website. This was the headline: SPACE CENTER HOUSTON BREACHED! Oh, no no no no no. I snatched the phone from Kay, who was startled, and scrolled through the phone. It said that the officials had found a threat on social media, saying that somebody would destroy the space center. They closed off the place from visitors today. I was not happy. And by "not happy", I mean that I was so mad that I threw my fidgets from my box. A little explanation: My dad had given me a box of fidgets when I got into a fight with Carissa in 1st grade. She was being mean to... yup, you guessed it, McKayla because she fell in mud. It would calm me down whenever I was mad. ANYWAYS, Kay jumped up and told me to stop throwing things around, but I didn't listen. I was frustrated. We spent so much time planning for today, and some dumb person decided to come and RUIN IT! Somebody opened my door. It was my mom, who had a stunned face. I stopped abruptly, and put on a fake smile. She didn't look convinced. "Calliope," she asked, tentatively, "Why are you throwing things across your room?" Awkward. "Um..." Kay saved us from being blasted to oblivion. "She saw a hate post from Carissa, and she kinda crashed out." Thank god for BFFs who are AMAZING at lying. "Okay," Mom said, "Make sure to tell me, next time that happens, instead of throwing your toys around, okay?" "Yes ma'am," I said, almost immediately. My mom walks out, closing the door. Kay and I collectively sigh.

"Be grateful that I have a plan for everything," Kay said, playfully hitting my arm. "Ow," I muttered, "Thank you, ever grateful McKayla Grey Carson." "You didn't have to say my middle name too, bro!" she said, swatting my arm again. "But, we're SCREWED!" I yelled, falling face-first on my bed. This stumped Kay. She paced across my room. Then, her face brightened, and she looked at me with a smile on her face. That exact moment, something dawned on me. "Ms. A can manipulate the Fog!" we yelled together. "Huh," I said, "I guess great minds DO think alike." Kay just shrugged. "I don't know about you, but I sure have a great mind," she said with a smirk. "Shut up!" I yelped, smacking her arm playfully.

"I should call and ask Ms. Arnyam really quick," she said, dialing Ms. A's phone number as she walked out of the room. I counted to 627 until she came back inside. "She's ready," Kay told me with a nod. "Then, I'll call Chris, we'll have breakfast, and will be on our way," I said, dialing his number. Moments later... "Hey, Calli," said Chris' voice on my phone. "Hey, Chris," I answered. "You heard about the threat aimed at NASA?" "Yeah," I said, "But Kay and I have a plan." I told him our plan. "That's brilliant! You two will be the exact reason why we won't die," he joked. I laughed, "Just tell me if you trust in our plan enough to come along."

"Hey," he said, his voice getting serious, "to quote a singular, somewhat smart person, 'You are now my friend, and I, for one, am not a person who doesn't trust a friend.'" It took me a second to realize that he was quoting me. "If you are done goofing around, come over, with permission, for breakfast. Ms. A's picking us up from my house." "Alright, alright, no need to get bossy," he said, hanging up. I turned to Kay, who was smirking. "What?" I asked in annoyance. "Nothing," she said, still smirking. "What did he say?" "What do you think he said, Kay. He said that he will come over for breakfast." Just as I replied to her, the doorbell rang. "Calli!" my mom called, "Chris and Mr. Campbell are here! They are ready to go!" Oh, god. I hadn't dressed yet! And Chris was already here, waiting.

I ran to my closet and got dressed. I wore a light magenta NASA tee and blue jeans; nothing special. I put my hair up in a high ponytail. Kay didn't need to rush like I did; she had gotten dressed while I was downstairs with my mom. She was wearing jeans overalls and a green t- shirt inside. She had her hair down and had a headband on to keep her curls from her face. We both raced to the kitchen, and found Chris and his dad, Mr. Campbell. He had dark brown hair, on top of it was an Astros hat (probably trying to fit in). His skin matched Chris', which was a sandy color. His eyes were caramel brown, unlike Chris', which were dark chocolate brown. "Hello," Mr. Campbell said. "I am Carlos Campbell, Chris' father." "Hey," said Chris, waving.

Kay and I waved back with a smile on our faces. It looked like we JUST might be able to pull this off! "Hi," I said, channeling my 'sweet girl' voice. "My name is Calli, short for Calliope and this is-" "McKayla. Or you could call me Kay, I don't mind any," interrupted Kay. "Nice to meet you, girls." "I am Cyrene Canderine, Calliope's mother," Mom said. "Nice to meet you too, ma'am. I assume that you guys are going to Space Center Houston, am I right?" We nodded. "Okay, then. Chris can stay here until your photography teacher can come to pick you up, is that okay?" We all nodded in affirmation. "Thank you," he said, turning to Chris. "I'll come to pick you up, whenever you come back, alright?"

Chris nodded, clearly relieved. "Goodbye. Nice to meet you guys!" he said as he walked out the front door. Once he left, we all breathed in relief. "Great. Now all we have to do is wait for Ms. A, yes?" Chris asked us. "Yeah," Kay and I replied together. My mom told us that there was food on the dining table. We ran to the dining room, and found soufflés and crepés on the table, along with exotic fruits such as dragon fruit (my personal fav) and passion fruit. So that's what my mom meant when she said she was making something special for us! All three of us stuffed the food down our throats. It was delicious. Ding dong. That was our cue to pack up and leave. Honestly? I was kind of scared to leave, knowing that I may not come back ever again.

Before I left, I gave my mom a huge hug, taking her by surprise. But she slowly melted into the hug, kissing the top of my head. "Bye, Mom," I told her, pecking her cheek. Right as I left the front door, I turned and looked at my mom. She may have changed through the years, but she looked the same. She still had the dark grey eyes, the dark, wavy hair, and the pink lips. Our house was still the same, too, with all its vintage furniture, which my dad had insisted on buying. [Warning, the next line may shock you] "I love you, Mom," I told my mother, somebody I despised ever since Dad died. Her eyes widened with shock, her mouth morphing into a smile. "I love you, too, sweetheart." Bitterly thinking that those were the last words I would hear from my mother, I sat into Ms. A— I mean Raya's white Hyundai Palisade.

Gosh, I need to remember not to call her Ms. A instead of Raya... "Hey, you guys!" greeted Raya. "Hey, Raya," we all said simultaneously. "You ready?" We shrugged as Chris pulled out mint cookies from his backpack and started eating them. I gave him a look of annoyance, but he just smirked and offered one to me. As we zoomed on the highway, my mind concluded: *Our quest had officially begun.*

Chapter 18- Kay Gets a Power-Up

Chapter 18- Kay Gets a Power-Up

After an hour of pep talk (none of which helped), we finally arrived at our destination. The entire area was crowded with security and police. We all looked at Raya, silently telling her to do her thing. She understood and, after getting out of the car, she closed her eyes in concentration. Suddenly, a powerful gust of wind blew from our direction, flooding the area. *The Fog,* I thought. It must've been so cool to control such a strong force, something that could alter people's memories. Soon, Raya put her chin up and started walking as if she owned the place. Kay, Chris, and I just followed her, trying to imitate. As we passed guards, they saluted us, or they bowed.

"I'm guessing they think we are their bosses?" I asked. Raya nodded. "Let's walk a bit faster. I don't think I can do this much longer."

We quickened our pace, and soon, we were welcomed inside the building. "Woah," Chris said. I agreed. Woah. I didn't remember seeing these things here, back then. But, as I said earlier, I was only 8, and I have a horrible memory. There were so many things to do there! They had this Mars Mission thing, they had multiple souvenir shops, and I can't forget the huge screen which greets us when we enter. It had slideshows on, showing the different things we could discover there. A sign to our right let us know that the auditorium was to our right, there was a crafting activity upstairs, and there was an exhibition of rockets and missions. I silently wished that there wouldn't be anything about my dad, or I would start crying. "Alright, gang," said Kay, "This is it." The rest of us just turned to her in annoyance. We seriously didn't want to know that we were on our quest for real. "Sorry," she mumbled. I turn around, looking for a "staff only" sign. Then, something caught my eye. "The tram- thingy is over there," I told my friends, pointing at the sign. "Will we be able to go on it, though?" Chris asked, turning to Raya. She shook her head. "I drained too much of my energy already. I don't know if I can use up more." Just as she said that, she looked like she remembered something. She took off her pack and rummaged through it. Soon, she pulled out a canteen and a Ziploc bag. "Here are some god- level healing supplies," she said.

She lifted the canteen. "This is the drink of the gods, nectar. Only use it in small amounts, since it may cause you to self-combust." Then, she lifted the Ziploc bag. "This is the food of the gods, ambrosia. Same directions as the nectar, use in small amounts." A thought struck me like lightning. "You said 'god- level healing supplies', right?" I asked Raya. She nodded, breaking a bit off the ambrosia and eating it. "Will Kay be able to eat this too? Since she is completely mortal?" Raya and Kay shared a glance, which kind of troubled me. Had they 2 secretly been talking? Finally, Raya said, "McKayla and I had just figured this out during her class on Friday. My dear, if you would please."

Kay closed her eyes firmly, and a scent filled the area. A flowery scent, followed by the smell of dirt. After that moment passed, she would've bit the dirt if I hadn't caught her. "K-k-Kay?" I asked, confused. "What was that?" "Descendant of Demeter," said Raya. "Ms. Carson is a grandchild of the Greek goddess of harvest and agriculture."

⬚ *Chapter 19 - I Got the Kay-Virus*

Chapter 19- I Got the Kay-Virus

My eyes widened with surprise. "How did y'all find out?" I asked Kay letting her sit down. "I was able to c-c-convince my p-parents to tell me on the phone," she said quietly, also stammering. "It's on my dad's side," she continued, her face pale. "Raya," I said cautiously, "why is Kay looking so pale?" Even Chris looked concerned. "I think it's the strain from using her power, even though she isn't properly trained." "Thanks," said Kay, her face turning to its normal color. I hadn't realized, but my hands, as if they had a mind of their own, took the baggie of

ambrosia from Raya and gave a piece to McKayla. "No prob," I said, trying to convince them that I meant to do that. Raya and Chris looked convinced. Kay, who knew me infinitely better than they, wasn't. "We should get going," I said, pulling McKayla up. Our group advanced towards the train ride. Kay was looking at me strangely, which worried me. It looked like she knew what happened with the ambrosia or something. Not that I knew any more than her.

Chapter 20- The Tram Ride (and Name-Calling)

Chapter 20- The Tram Ride (and Name-Calling)

We kept on walking towards the tram. Kay was still staring at me weirdly, and Raya and Chris were as oblivious as ever. There were some guards at the doors, who opened the door for us, bowing. I put my chin up and kept on walking with my friends. God, I could get used to this treatment. "My dear guests, may I do you the favour of driving the tram?" said a voice behind us. All four of us turned simultaneously. Raya was the fastest one to recover. "Of course! We would be grateful if you would," she said with charm. I think she has a bit of Aphrodite blood in her, don't you think? The man was a security guard, who nodded as he walked towards the front of the tram. He pulled out the keys, and the engine roared to life. We all climbed to the back of the train, which was the closest to us and the best place to strategize (as if we had anything else to plan). The tram lurched forwards, and took a u- turn to this tunnel. Oh! I remembered this! It led to different facilities which worked for NASA.

It was pretty quiet, so McKayla the Chatterbox spoke up. "Alright, I'll bite. Where will we find the lowest point? This place is huge!" Chris smiled, causing my stomach to go into a frenzy. "Why are you smiling, Chris the Clown?" I asked skeptically. He slowly pulled out a flyer/pamphlet of some sort. "This is why I'm smiling, Calli the Captain. I pickpocketed one of the security guards. He was probably new, because he had a pretty detailed map of the entire area."

It was pretty detailed, I'll grant him that, but calling me the captain? That was crazy! And it was aimed as a way to tease me, not a compliment.

I didn't say any of that, though, just fumed on the fact that he called me CAPTAIN! As if I need to know everything my 'crew' knows! Both Kay and Raya stared at us, noticing the new development.

I individually gave both of them the side-eye, and they concentrated on the pamphlet. Raya pointed to something called the 'Astronaut Training Facility.' "There," she said. "I think there is some type of basement there." She was right. There was a door labeled 'basement'. "So, I guess we will go there," said Chris the Clown. And yes, he will be called that by me until I get over it.

Raya nodded. "And that is also where I will depart, and Calliope will lead y'all into the Underworld."

I looked down. I didn't want all the responsibility on my shoulders. If something happened to my friends, I would never forgive myself. Despite what Chris called me, I was nowhere near a 'captain'. Kay noticed my distress and placed her hand on my shoulder. "Hey," she said calmly, "You aren't alone." "Yeah," said Chris, "Even though you act like the captain or leader of the group, we'll be here for you."

I gave Chris the stink eye. Even his attempts to be reassuring seemed like teasing. Despite that... "Thanks, you guys," I said. And I meant it.

I mean, I practically lived with Kay, and she always calms me down. And Chris, well, even though he's annoying, he still trusted me with his heritage and his past, and I'm truly grateful for that. "We have arrived at the Astronaut Training Facility. Please make sure to watch your step, and a guide will meet you at the door, possibly," said the guard on the speaker.

Chapter 21- We Say Bye to the Best Teacher Ever

Chapter 21- We Say Bye to the Best Teacher Ever

Wow. It looked like luck was on our side. We arrived at the exact building we needed to enter. "So," said Raya, "This is where we separate, kids." I'll admit, I wasn't ready for her to leave. But we had discussed this. She would distract security while we broke in.

I went and hugged Ms. Arnyam. I didn't have anything better to give her, so a hug had to do. I was really glad that she had helped us so much. I'll also admit this, because Kay won't: McKayla got teary-eyed. She hated saying goodbye, but she never explained why.

After Kay's waterworks, Chris gave Raya a bear hug, which he was surprisingly capable of. "Okay, okay, you three softies," Raya said, pulling away from Chris. She ran her delicate fingers through my hair. "Go save your mother's magic, alright?"

I nodded. Ms. Arnyam turned around and concentrated on altering the guards' minds. It must've taken a lot of strength, because there were so many guards. I looked at my friends, who were, like me, staring at Raya doing her magic. She was good. The guard next to the door unlocked it and let us inside the building.

Chapter 22- Oops, I Did it Again :)

Chapter 22- Oops, I Did it Again :)

Now, if you have been to the Astronaut Training Facility from the tram, you went up the stairs and into a glass corridor, right? But, thanks to the Fog, the security guard (whose nametag said Timothy Hudson) led us straight into the actual training area, the one you see from the glass up there. It was empty, I realized. "Probably from the threat," whispered Kay in my right ear. Great. Not only can my best friend bring nature wherever she goes, but she can also read my thoughts. Where is privacy these days?! If not for Mr. Hudson (or something), we would've gotten lost in all the equipment here.

Chris and Kay were amazed; you could see it in their eyes. I guess they haven't been somewhere like this. I haven't either, and I was pretty amazed too, but I know how to hide my expressions. I felt a tug on my hand. "There," Chris whispered. It was loud enough for Kay to hear on the other side of me, but it was quiet enough for Mr. Hudson not to hear. There it was. A door labeled basement. But there was another thing written on the silver plaque: Authorized Personnel Only. We qualified as 'Authorized Personnel', right?? (Don't dash my hopes, dear reader. I know we qualify!) "How do we distract him?" Kay asked quietly. I got to thinking. Then, finally, I got an idea. I didn't consult Kay or Chris before doing this, so we all know what will happen.

After signalling my friends to go on, I stopped, and aimed my right hand towards the glass hallway where the visitors gawk at the workers. I thought about all the resentment I held for Carissa, for Hades, for life in general, and I imagined it all going into my palm. I closed my eyes and concentrated. That was the last thing I remembered from then. Later, Kay and Chris told me what happened. Kay, being the concerned best friend, stayed back and watched me shoot the black light of doom towards the glass. It exploded in a very large kaboom! According to McKayla, my eyes turned purple, not the lilac type, but the dark type; the one you would associate with Halloween and stuff like that. The air grew cold. Now, back to when I started remembering. Mr. Hudson ran towards the staircase, completely ignoring the fact that I had fallen flat on the floor, tendrils of smoke coming out of my palm. Kay ran towards me, her face tight with concern. "Are you alright?" she asked, checking me for injuries like the good friend she is. Chris also came, asking about my well-being. I just showed a thumbs-up, but I used my right hand, which hurt badly. "Chris, get the things Raya gave us from her pack," said Kay. Huh? I thought distantly. What things? Chris zipped open my bag and brought out the Ziploc bag with, what did Raya call it... Ambrosia and the canteen of nectar. Oh, I thought, those things! "Guys," I said weakly, "The door." Their eyes widened with surprise, as if they forgot everything but me and whatever I did back there. They know their priorities, do they not?

Chris and Kay helped me get up, but after giving me an ambrosia square and a swig of nectar. For all of y'all's burning questions, ambrosia tasted like the dragon fruit my mom gave us before we left, and the nectar tasted like this Greek yogurt drink my dad used to make for me when I was younger. It had dragon fruit (again, it's my favorite), grapes, and strawberry Greek yogurt. I felt a twinge of sadness. My mom must be so worried for me, since I was practically her only family (other than Hades) left. Also, I hadn't tasted Froúto giaoúrti (As my dad would call it) since I was eight. Back to my dear, helpful friends, Kay took my left arm, and Chris took my right and they both looped my arm around their necks. "How are we going to unlock this door?" Chris said. Kay smiled. What is wrong with my friends smiling during horrid situations?!

"Looks like Chris isn't the only one who can pickpocket guards," said Kay with a smirk, pulling an access card from her overalls' pocket. "Dude," said Chris, "Leave the stealing to me, you copycat!" "Sorry, I had too!" joked Kay with a smile. I love my friends, even if they both liked smuggling things from security guards. She tapped the card on the reader. It was like the world held its breath. *Welcome, Mr. Timothy Hudson,* it said in a robotic voice, granting us access. "Let's go!" Chris said, pumping his right fist. Our little trio limped into the dark cavern. Now, this is where things get interesting.

Chapter 23- Kay Tries to Kill Me (Not Really)

Chapter 23- Kay Tries to Kill Me (Not Really)

I have to emphasize the fact that the Underworld isn't a fun place. I mean, the walk itself to the Underworld stank. Thankfully, Kay was able to use a bit of her flower power to make the tunnel smell like Hibiscus. Our group was silent, which worried me. Kay was the most talkative person I had ever met, and Chris talked a lot. Even I was silent, which also scared me. I talk more when I'm nervous, which I was very much. "So," I said, breaking the silence," We should talk to, like, you know, help us be ready for the Underworld." It was their turn to look at me in annoyance. Not a good sign. Kay barely gets annoyed.

"Let's stop here, for a while," McKayla said after an eternity of crickets. I hadn't realized that my friends must be tired after hoisting me up for so long. "Sorry," I said quietly. "It's alright," Kay said, smiling. Chris was rummaging through his bag. He smiled while bringing something out. A flashlight, I thought, wondering why I hadn't brought one. Thankfully, the batteries still worked. The light shining from the flashlight helped us see better. Suddenly, Kay stumbled forward. "Oh my god!" I yelled, frantically trying to hold her up. "Chris, find something which Kay can sit on!" I told Chris, who nodded and helped me bring Kay to a stone slab. "Hey," I said quietly," I need you to talk to me."

McKayla's face was pale. She didn't say anything. "It must be from the strain of holding you up and making the tunnel smell like flowers," Chris said, force feeding her ambrosia. I felt horrible. I was the one who told her to make the tunnel smell like flowers, and I was the person she was trying to lift. Thankfully, after the multiple doses of ambrosia, she was able to sit up. She still looked sickly, but she was alright. I gave her a hug, which she rapidly melted into. Then, I slapped her arm. "If you ever do that to me again, I will kill you," I said in a serious tone. Kay had the nerve to laugh. "Sorry." "Dude, I should be the one to say sorry. To both of you," I said, turning to Chris. "Kay, you had us worried!" Chris said, giving her some nectar. "Thanks. And sorry," she said weakly. "You better be!" she flinched at my voice.

"I was sooo scared and anxious. I thought you left me-" I said, my voice cracking. I sat down on the ground and put my face in my hands as tears started falling. I was really frustrated, if you couldn't guess. I mean, did you blame me? My best friend, who was helping me, fainted because of me! I hated myself at that moment. I also decided that I would never let anything like this happen ever again. "Hey, Calli," Kay said. "I'm alright! See!" I lifted my head out of my hands only to see McKayla, who was unconscious a second ago, doing a cartwheel! I quickly stood up. "Now you're trying to give me a heart attack, Kay," I said in an annoyed tone. But I couldn't help the smile widening on my face. There was the girl I grew up with. "See," she said with a smirk on her face. "I can make anybody happy!"

"Even the grumpy, impromptu captain of our group," said Chris with a grin on his face. "Oh, shut up!" I said, pushing him playfully. Then we just sat down on the slab, our stomachs hurting from laughing so hard. Kay gave me a side hug. "Sorry to scare you, bro," she said. "It's alright, I guess," I said with a shrug. "But I will follow up on my threat if you do it again!" She just laughed. Again. God, I need to be more intimidating! "Alright, alright," Chris said, standing up. "We should get going." Kay and I nodded as we gathered our things and got up. Chris was about 3 yards away from us and was staring at where the flashlight was pointing. "Guys," he said cautiously, "You have to come see this."

We quickly went to him and realized why he was staring. We're in the Underworld now.

Chapter 24- Hello, Divine Help

Chapter 24- Hello, Divine Help

When you hear somebody say 'the Underworld', you may imagine a very dark landscape with ghosts everywhere. You are, to some extent, correct, but there is more. When our group arrived, we were all awestruck. Yes, it was very dark, and yes, ghosts were roaming around. We saw a huge, pitch black river. I knew exactly what it was. "The River Styx," I told my friends, who still haven't recovered from the shock. There were other things, of course. For example, we saw a meadow with ghosts just standing around, doing nothing. That was the Asphodel Meadows. The souls who didn't do much in life were sent there.

Then, we saw this magnificent field. There were many beautiful houses, and the souls there looked happy. That was Elysium, where the souls who did good deeds in life went. In the center of Elysium, though, there was a lake of some sort with an island in the middle. That was the Isle of the Blessed. If you had achieved Elysium 3 times (after rebirth), then you would go there. It was like heaven in heaven, you know? We, then, saw the Fields of Punishment, where the wicked souls went to serve jail time. "This place is giving me the creeps," said Kay. "Of course, this place will give you the creeps, Kay," I said. "We're in the Underworld now!" "Are you getting the creeps, Captain?" Chris asked. Honestly? I felt better than I had ever felt before. I think it was because of the Hades part of me, but still. I felt good. After a long time, I encountered strength. But I didn't say any of that. Instead, I shrugged. My friends didn't look convinced. It's alright. They didn't have to. "Now, how are we going to cross this river?" I asked, trying to change the topic. Right as I said that, I heard footsteps behind me. "Looks like you could use some help." We turned to see this young man with wings on his shoes and sprouting out from his hat. In his hand, he had some sort of stick with snakes curling around it. "Wait," Kay said with a determined look on her face. "I know who you are!" When we all waited for her to speak, she said," Wait, it will come to me!" An eternity later, her brain caught up as she said, "Hermes. The god of messengers." Hermes chuckled as he bowed.

"The name is Hermes, young lady. And I get it, you three are Calliope Canderine, Chris Campbell, and McKayla Carson?" he said, pointing to each of us as he spoke our names. "How do you know our names?" I asked tentatively. He laughed once more. "Don't forget, dear, I'm the god of messengers, so I make it my mission to keep up with all the drama." I raised an eyebrow. Drama? "Oh," he said quickly. "I didn't tell you kids about what's going on in Olympus. Demeter and Aphrodite are trying to convince Zeus to stop you guys from confronting Hades." "What?!" the three of us said in unison. "Why?" I asked, ginger building up inside of me. Hermes smiled, clearly glad that I was that agitated.

"Well, because, darling, Demeter and Aphrodite think that Hades is going to pulverize their grandchildren, just as he will do to you." I was stunned. Hades won't pulverize me, right? "Now, now," Hermes continued, "I am here to help. After all, I was considered the protector of travelers." We sighed in relief. We all knew having a god on our side was a good thing. "But," he said, shattering our hopes, "There is a catch." I groaned and rolled my eyes. I hated catches. "I can only lead you across the river and through the judgment area, but after that, Zeus or Hades may find out that I was here." Thank god, he would do something! "Thank you, Lord Hermes," I said with a curtsy. My friends followed.

"Alright, this way, folks!" Hermes said cheerfully. He closed his eyes, and his caduceus (that's the word I was looking for!) turned into a boat. "Hop in, kids!" he said, helping each of us into the boat. He also gave us earplugs. "To block out the sound of the Acheron, kid," he told Chris when he questioned. While crossing the Acheron, the river of pain, I had time to think about what Hermes told us. About how Chris and Kay's grandmothers didn't want them to face Hades for fear that they would get turned to dust, like Hades would do to me. Supposedly. *You want to pulverize me, Hades? I thought angrily. Then, bring it on.*

🎁 Chapter 25- We Get Late/ Early Birthday Gifts

Chapter 25- We Get Late/ Early Birthday Gifts

"So," Hermes said as we got off the boat and took out our earbuds, "This way to the doors to the Underworld!" Doors? Did he not mean a gigantic gateway that made the Gateway Arch look tiny? No, like seriously, the entryway was ginormous! It was pitch black, which reminded me of my dad's eyes. (I know, I know. I chided myself silently after that thought.) There were 3 lines: one leading to Elysium, one going to the Asphodel Meadows, and the last one going to the Fields of Punishment. Hermes led us to the line going to Elysium. As we walked through, I felt like I was home.

I would be the strongest here. And I would, considering how energized I felt since we entered. "I don't think I should be here," Kay whispered in my ear. She sounded sick, again. "Of course you aren't. The granddaughter of Demeter in the Underworld? You grow plants and stuff. Have you seen any here? Also," I continued, "You know the story of Persephone, your aunt of some sort, and Hades, right?" She nodded. "Of course I know," she said, "I was just saying because we were so quiet." "Sorry," I said, feeling guilty. She gave me a thumbs-up and swung her arm around me. Soon after that, I heard a howling sound. "Guys," Chris said, "Did y'all just hear Cerberus, or is that just me?"

"Of course it's Cerberus, darling," Hermes assured. "But don't worry. I have a chew toy for each of its heads!" I don't think Chris was persuaded. If Hermes turned around and saw his face, he would see it too. For all of y'all who haven't been to the Underworld or met

Cerberus, it is actually adorable. My old neighbor had a dog, and I would play with it a lot. So, in short, I loved dogs. My dog-lover part of my brain thought Cerberus was adorable, but the sane part of it (which had reduced to 15% of my brain) thought it was scary and was going to gobble us up. Hermes conjured some dog toys and threw them to each of the heads with perfect accuracy. You'd think he was the god of archery. He did it so quickly that we hadn't even realized that this was where he would go back.

"So, children, this is where we go our separate ways," Hermes said with a sigh. "Thank you, Lord Hermes, for guiding us this far," I said with a bow. My friends copied. "You know what?" he said, "You three are good kids, I'll grant you that. I'll also put in a good word for you three to the Olympian

Council. And, for being amazing," he pulled out a satch from who knows where, "you get gifts!" Our eyes widened with surprise. Woah. That came out of nowhere. Hermes started handing out our 'gifts'. "For Ms. Carson, a gardening belt with seeds. For Mr. Campbell, a harp sword. Hope you can fight with a sword, kid," Hermes said, handing them their items. "And finally for Ms. Canderine. I heard along the grapevine that you had a knack for archery. So, I got you a bow and a quiver-full of arrows."

I was shocked once more. I barely told anyone about the archery classes I used to take in 5th grade. "Thank you," was all I could say to him. Hermes just smiled and vanished into the air. I turned and looked at my friends. "Let's go and give Hades a piece of our minds."

💀 Chapter 26- Kay Gets to Say 'I Told You So'

Chapter 26- Kay Gets to Say 'I Told You So'

We walked through Hades while trying out our new supplies. Chris had taken sword-fighting classes from his dad, so he didn't have any trouble with the harpe. "Oh my god, this thing is amazing!" Kay exclaimed, examining every pouch. I was running my hands over the smooth wood of the bow and sliding my fingers up and down the bow string. It was beautiful. There were carvings on the wooden part. There were symbols related to Hades, and some symbolizing magic. Then, my eyes came across an engraving. "You guys!" I told my friends, "Take a look at this." Kay put her seeds up, and Chris sheathed his sword as they followed my gaze. "C. M. E." I said.

"Calli," Kay said, "Aren't those your mom's maiden name initials?" I smiled. Cyrene Mellou Erato. "I guess Hermes stole from my mother," I said. "Now Hermes is copying me?" Chris asked, making us laugh. "I don't think Hermes will accept that, Clown," I said, using the nickname I have for him. He gave me the side-eye, making me laugh once again. God, what was wrong with me? Suddenly, McKayla stopped. "Kay," Chris asked, "Why are you stopping?" "I think something's following us. I've been hearing footsteps, but I couldn't find out where they came from." "I think you're just hallucinating," I told her. "This place must be affecting you the most, with the entire Demeter thing."

Kay didn't look assured, but she kept on walking. Abruptly, we heard the sound of whips behind us. We turned in sync to find three winged creatures, and an entire battalion of skeletons before us. The middle one stepped forward. "I take it you must be Calliope Canderine, yes?" she said in a raspy voice. I looked at my friends in alarm. I tried to look unafraid as I stepped forward as well. "And I take it you three must be the Furies, or the Erinyes, am I right?" I said a silent thank you to Kay for sending me that website all those days ago about Hades. She snarled. "You think you are very smart, don't you?" she asked in an angry tone. "Very well," she continued. "I am Alecto, the one on my left is Megaera, and on my right is Tisisphone. We are here on Hades' orders to bring you to the dungeons for disrespecting him." "Disrespect?" I asked. "What does he know about respect, then? Is it respectful to destroy my mom's work, which she did all to meet her father? Is it respectful to destroy a girl's life? Is it respectful to neglect your child?" I spoke through grinding teeth. "Calli," Kay said, placing her hand on my shoulder, "Calm down." I took a deep breath and took a step back. "You want us? Come and take us," I said. My Texas History teacher would be proud. Alecto growled as she signaled the skeletons to fight as she and her sisters flew away. They probably went to tell Hades about this predicament. I yelled in defiance as I shot an arrow at the nearest skeleton. My friends were quick to recover, thankfully, or they would've been skeleton chow. Chris unsheathed his sword and started to dislocate all of the skeletons' bones. Kay brought out her seeds and threw multiple on the ground. She concentrated, and soon, there were plants fighting alongside us. But our rush didn't last long. One of the skeletons was able to take my quiver from me, leaving me with a bow only. Chris' swings were getting slower, doing less damage, and Kay dropped all her seeds. My foot throbbed, probably because of the amount of pressure I was putting on it. McKayla's forehead was bleeding, and Chris lost his sword and twisted his arm. We were forced to make a defensive ring. From the corner of my eye, I saw McKayla stumbling. It looked like she was going to fall down any moment. I hated that Kay was that hurt. I closed my eyes and concentrated. "Chris, Kay," I warned, "Get behind me."

They listened without hesitation. I thought about Kay getting hurt, Chris injuring his arm. I thought about Raya, who had risked herself for this quest. But most importantly, I thought about my parents. I may have not seen my dad in a really long time, I knew that, if he was here, he wouldn't want me to fail. And my *mom, well, I was here because I wanted her to get her magic back. I poured my resentment into my palms, and faced them towards the army of skeletons trying to kill us. I roared as black light shot out of my palms, which disintegrated the corpses. I vaguely saw a winged figure around where Kay stood, but that didn't seem important at that time. I fell to the ground in exhaustion, blacking out. The last thing I heard was Kay screaming.*

☺ Chapter 27- Don't! Just Don't!

Chapter 27- Don't! Just Don't!

"Calli!" I faintly heard. I wake up on the ground, Chris holding me. "Woah, Captain," he said. "You had me worried "W- w- where's Kay?" I asked softly, trying to sit up. He sadly shook his head. "The Furies took her away, Calli."

I couldn't hold myself back anymore. My cries were soft and quiet, but quickly gained volume. I was sobbing uncontrollably. First my dad, then my mom's powers, now my best friend? Why do I keep getting things taken from me! Suddenly, I felt strong arms around me. It was Chris'. I cried on his shoulder, not knowing what to do.

Kay was right, I realized. She knew from the beginning that something bad would happen. It was I who didn't listen, but it was her who had to pay. Chris slowly pulled away, wiped a tear off my cheek, and tucked a strand of my hair behind my ear. I was dumbfounded. And I stared at those dark, chocolate brown eyes. And I wasn't even ready for his lips on mine. His breath smelled like mint, my favorite flavor of ice cream. As he pulled away once more, I was in shock. "Chris, I-" "Don't say anything," he interrupted. "Just don't." He started talking. "I know we recently met, and I know we don't know each other that well, but since that day on the bus, I was mesmerised, Calli. Something about you drew me closer to you until I couldn't help but love you. You were the first person that I told about my mom and Aphrodite. I just knew that I could trust you. I also knew that you were dealing with something really similar. If you don't feel the same, then don't-"

It was my turn to interrupt him.

I pulled him towards me and hugged him. I quickly pulled away, smiling. "So," I said, my voice hoarse, "I can't even say that I love you back?" His cheeks colored as he got up and gave me his hand. "Come on," he said.

I nodded, taking his hand. "We've got a friend to save."

🤬 CHAPTER 28- I REALLY START HATING HADES

Chapter 28- I Really Start Hating Hades

"So," I said, trying to break the silence, "Hades sent the furies to take Kay as leverage, yes?" Chris nodded. He hadn't said anything since, you know, what happened back there. "Dude," I said, stopping and getting in front of him, "You gotta say something!" "What do you want me to say?" he asked, his tone slightly annoyed. "It's not such a huge deal, you know? I understand! Heck, I kissed you back!!!" "I know that, Calli." "Then why are you so silent, like you're hiding something from me?" "I'm not," he said, sternly. "Well," I continued, "If you aren't, then say something which will change my mind!"

What happened to him? One second ago, he was pouring his heart out, and the next second, he was arguing with me! Chris lowered his head. "I was thinking about what Megaera said." That, once again, took me by surprise. "What did she say?" I asked, my tone soft. He sat down near a poplar tree and looked up with tears streaming down his face. "I'm scared, Calli. I didn't want you to know. But, I'm terrified." I sat down next to him. "Calm down," I said, imagining I was Kay and he was Calli, "It'll be alright." He gave a half- hearted laugh. "Does Kay tell that to you?" I smiled. "You know me pretty well, Clown." "I do, don't I, Captain?" I laughed.

"No, but like, seriously, what did she say?" His smile faded. "She said that she was taking McKayla away because that would be your punishment," he said, his voice barely heard. My mind was spinning. Megaera, I thought. "Megaera. Isn't she the one representing jealousy, envy, and grudges?" I asked Chris. He just shrugged. "I don't know. Do you know anything else about her? Or why she wanted to punish you?" It took me a while, but I came to a conclusion. "I told you about how I hated my mother after my dad died?" He nodded. "I told you why I hated her, right?" He nodded again. "It was because she kept on making you help her in finding your dad, yes?"

I nodded. "I think hating her like that could be considered a grudge..." His eyes widened. "Of course! Hades must've known about your resentment for your mother, and he probably told the Fu-" "Call them the Kindly Ones. So we don't alert them," I interrupted. "-the Kindly Ones so they could come after you," Chris finished. He stood up, but faltered. He would have face- planted on the ground if I didn't catch him. "Woah," I said, concern creeping into my voice. "Sit while I get you some ambrosia and nectar." He slightly nodded as I set him down on the ground. I pulled out the supplies from my backpack and gave it to him. Then, I examined his arm, which was turning purple. "Chris, you should've told me about your arm," I said.

"There's a first- aid kit in my backpack," he said, weakly. I took the kit from his bag. Inside, there were the supplies I needed to immobilize his arm: an ice pack, some bandaging wrap, and ibuprofen. I gave him the ibuprofen and a bottle of water to wash it down. I wrapped the ice pack in a cloth and placed it where his skin was turning purple. I, then, bandaged the arm and tried to create a sling of some sort. (It worked, if you can believe it.) In about ten minutes, Chris was ready to go, with his arm in a sling and multiple doses of ambrosia and nectar. "Thanks, Captain," he said with a smile. I smiled back, oblivious to the fact that he called me Captain again. God, what's wrong with me? "Come on, Clown," I said. "Kay's waiting on us."

We started towards Hades' palace, walking side by side. "Hey," Chris said quietly. I look at him in confusion. "Sorry for being so awkward with you since, you know..." he trailed off. "It's alright," I said with a grin." If I were in your place, the info the Kindly One gave you in my head, I would act the same." He smiled and put out his arms. I stepped towards him and hugged him. There were butterflies the size of blue whales in my stomach, but I tried to push them aside. He slowly pulled away. "Thanks," he said.

I gently swatted his arm. "You don't need to say thanks for that, you know?" "Now that I think of it," he said a while later, "You really aren't such a Captain, but more of a comforter."

I laughed. "Me? A comforter? I think you've mistaken me for McKayla. She's the one who gives everybody solace. I'm, most of the time, the reason why people need solace." He snorted. "I really can't see you being unpleasant to people, unless they have made you mad." "But still," he continued, "Even though you aren't such a captain, I will keep on calling you that." I gave him the side-eye. "And you can still call me the Clown," he added, "If you want to." I smiled. "Since I haven't changed my mind, I will stick to calling you a Clown, thank you very much." "Let's not get off task," Chris said. I nodded. "Kay is waiting for us." And so is my wrath on Hades.

Chapter 29- We Get Jump- Scared

Chapter 29- We Get Jump- Scared

We trudged through the Underworld, taking in the dreary scenery. We had to walk around the Fields of Punishment. And, yes, that's what I meant when I said 'dreary'. We saw Sisyphus rolling a rock uphill, and we heard him yelling from pretty far away. By yelling, I mean cussing out in, like, 10 different languages. Do you blame him, though? If I were in his place, I would be screaming too. Then, Chris drew his sword, pointing its tip at the Palace a lā Hades. If I had to give an award to the gloomiest place in the Underworld, it would have to go to Hades' gates. I mean, there were these horrifying depictions of wars, famines, and bombings. If these pictures are from modern times, I thought distantly, then why do they look like they were engraved a long time ago?

"So," I said, looking at the closed gates, "How do we get in?" "We could use your disintegrating power," Chris answered. I nodded. "But, whenever I do use it, I go too far and get myself, and possibly others, hurt." That stumped Chris. Then, his eyes widened, as if he had an idea. "You could use a little bit, you know?" he said finally. I cocked my head to the side. "Here," Chris said, "How about this. Hypothetically, let's say that you need to think of something that you resent, and that resentment turns into the black light that shines from your hands. So, you could think about things that don't really make you mad, but are still on that list. Then, the amount of anger that thing causes, that's the strength of your dark light power! How do you like my explanation?" I was stunned. And coming up with that plan only took, like, 2 minutes. He was good. When I finally came to my senses, I replied, "That only took you 2 minutes to come up with?" He nodded. I laughed. "Bro! How did you know I was actually thinking about things I resent, and then those thoughts became my power?!" Chris was shocked. "I, uh, it's an Aphrodite thing," he said. I gestured to him to keep on talking. "I can read people's emotions, so whenever you used that power thing, I felt a wave of resentment flooding through the area." I smiled. "That means what you planned could work." "Now, what are we waiting for?" Chris asked. "Do it!"

I closed my eyes and envisioned my 2nd-grade teacher. I was in second grade when my dad died, so the kids in the class loved to make fun of me, and Ms. Jenkins did nothing about it. She was a nice teacher, but she still made me mad. I imagined my resentment going to my right palm, which was grabbing the gate. The gate exploded in a tiny boom! "I owe you soda," I told Chris, while sprinting inside the now obliterated gates. He followed. We entered a beautiful garden. There were bushes with rubies and trees with diamonds. But the prettiest of them all was the pomegranate tree, full of the ripest ones I have ever seen. "Persephone's garden," Chris said. "Don't eat anything unless you want to stay in the Underworld forever," I warned him, just as he reached for a pom. He quickly recoiled, taking what I said into account.

"Who DARES to enter my garden!" demands a voice behind us. We turn to face Persephone, the Queen of the Underworld, and the Goddess of Springtime.

Chapter 30 - Hello, Divine Help 2.0

Chapter 30- Hello, Divine Help 2.0

Persephone wasn't just beautiful. She was beautiful. It probably won't make sense to y'all because you haven't ever seen her, but you should. It will change your entire perspective on beauty. Anyways, back to the Goddess of Springtime. Persephone had lustrous, long, dark hair, and warm brown eyes that reminded me of melting chocolate in a s'more (The amount of people I know with eyes like chocolate is crazy: Chris, Mr. Campbell, Persephone, etc). She was tall and radiated elegance. She was wearing a flowing gown decorated with flowers. She also had fair skin. I realized that I was gawking, so I quickly nudged Chris to stop as well.

"I don't think I was clear," Persephone said. "What are you doing in my garden?" I quickly recovered. "Greetings, my lady," I said, bowing deeply. "We are here to meet Hades and rescue our friend, whom he took unfairly." She laughed gently. It was a beautiful sound. "Oh, you must be Calliope Canderine, right?" I slowly nodded. "My gods, your mother, my step-daughter, made my lord pretty mad, you know?" she said with a smile. "Um, if you don't mind," Chris butted in, "We would be really grateful if you allowed us inside the palace. Without hurting us, of course." Persephone laughed once more. "Why would I hurt you? You and your friends are really brave; brave enough to venture to the Underworld, away from the Sun!"

We both sighed in relief. Thank goodness, another god on our side. This time, somebody who can help us convince Hades! "Thank you, Lady Persephone," I said, curtsying again, this time Chris bowing alongside me. "I heard about what my lord did to your mother's magic, Calliope," she said. "And, I can help you get it back." I smile widely. "I don't know how I can thank you, my lady." "No need," Persephone said. "Now, come along. He is in the throne room. I shall guide you there." She waved her hand, and we were whisked away into the throne room of Hades.

Chapter 31- The Throne Room of Hades

Chapter 31- The Throne Room of Hades

Persephone had teleported us to the grand throne room of Hades, my interesting grandfather. (Interesting being a code word for multiple curses I am not allowed to say...) The room was huge, but it was expected, for somebody so important like the God of the Underworld. His throne was obsidian black, engraved with his symbols, like skulls and pomegranates. Hades was sitting on the throne. He had shoulder-length black hair and ebony-black eyes. He also had a long, black beard. He was wearing a dark robe and had a wedding ring on his left hand. "What are you doing here, Granddaughter?" Hades asked in a booming voice.

I looked up at him with anger in my eyes. "You very well know what I am doing here, Hades." Chris put his hand on my shoulder. "Calm down, Calli." I shrugged him off. "How dare you take away my mom's magic and ruin my life!?" I yelled, walking towards him and notching an arrow. "Calli!" yelled a familiar voice to my right. I momentarily put my bow and arrow down and found the person who yelled my name. It was Kay, her overalls battered, her forehead bandaged up. She was chained to a column near a World War 2 soldier. She had tiny cuts on her exposed arms and had tears in her eyes. "Kay!" I yelled, running towards her just as the soldier stepped in front of Kay, blocking her.

I faced Hades. "You have a problem with my mom, right?" His eyes narrowed. "Then let McKayla go back home with Chris. They are only endangered because of me, and that won't be true any longer!" "Calli!" McKayla said, "What are you doing, you ding-dong!" I turned to face my best friend. Then, I turned to Chris, whom I secretly liked. I turned back to Kay. "There have been too many occasions where you or Chris have gotten hurt for me. I don't want you two to be in danger anymore. This is my fight, and I need you two to go away." "Let the girl go," Hades commanded the soldier, who unbounded Kay as she ran to me and gave me a huge hug. "I knew you would come for me, Calli," she whispered in my ear.

I pulled away. "Kay, you need to take Chris and get out of here." She shook her head. "Never. This isn't just your fight, Calli. This is our fight. We're in this together, right?!" Chris ran towards us, wrapping us both in a hug. "Captain, we aren't leaving you. Not when you need us most," he said. I smiled. I loved these two pickpockets. Chris and McKayla turned to Hades, and I searched the room for Persephone. I couldn't find her, so I turned to Hades alongside my friends. I yelled in defiance, and we charged on a very surprised God of the Dead. In my head, I realized I couldn't go down with people better than those two; McKayla Carson, my best friend and surrogate sister, the one person who has been by my side for as long as I can remember. Chris Campbell, my other best friend, somebody who's in love with me (and vice versa), the person who has the most trust in me than anybody else. My two best friends. Before we could go any closer, somebody stopped us. She had dark, luscious hair and chocolate eyes. Persephone, I thought distantly. "Stop!" she commanded, and the entire room froze...

Chapter 32- I Become Reckless

Chapter 32- I Become Reckless

"Do you mortals think you can fight Hades and come out alive?" she asked us. "Are you that stupid?!" I got mad. "Aren't you supposed to help us?" I yelled back at Persephone. "I am helping you," she said, "By advising you not to fight Hades." Kay put her hand on my shoulder. "Stop, Calli. You're being reckless." I glared at her, and she glared back at me, which was strange. McKayla never lost her temper, unlike me. She had a mysterious sort of fire in her hazel eyes. I lowered my gaze and relaxed my tense shoulders. She nodded and removed her hand. "What are we supposed to do, if we aren't going to fight him?" Chris asked the goddess. Hades cleared his throat.

"Let them fight me," he said to his wife. "I will happily disintegrate them." "No, my lord," she replied, "I will not allow these valiant heroes charge off to their death." "Persephone, you are going to let the puny children fight me, or you will face consequences." Her face paled, but she stepped away from us. I looked at my friends standing beside me. I drew an arrow, and we ran towards Hades. He got up from his throne and turned to a normal sized human, yelling in anger. "Guards!" he screamed, commanding them to fight us. Kay and Chris fought the soldiers around Hades, while I took the god himself. "You think you, a grandchild of a god, can beat me in a fight?" he asked while shooting me with a dark light from his staff.

I smirked. "Yes, I do, thank you very much," I replied, just as one of my arrows sank into his arm. He yelled in pain as golden liquid came out from the wound. Ichor, I thought, the blood of gods. I closed my eyes, and imagined everything that could fuel my power. I screamed, and dark light shot from my hand and went through Hades' armor. But, he recovered shortly and hit my right shin with his dark power, burning away part of my jeans. I fell to one knee. My foot was burning. He had hit right where the alligator had bit me all those years ago, the scar that was still there even after 7 years. My eyes watered, as Hades raised his staff above me. "Finally," he said in triumph, "You will realize not to mess with Hades!" Just before he could strike me with his staff, somebody stopped it, using their hand.

It was a feminine hand, with a quartz ring on her ring finger. "Father," she said in a dangerous tone, her voice all too familiar, "Get. Away. From. My. Daughter." I raised my eyes, to find my mother grabbing Hades' staff to protect me.

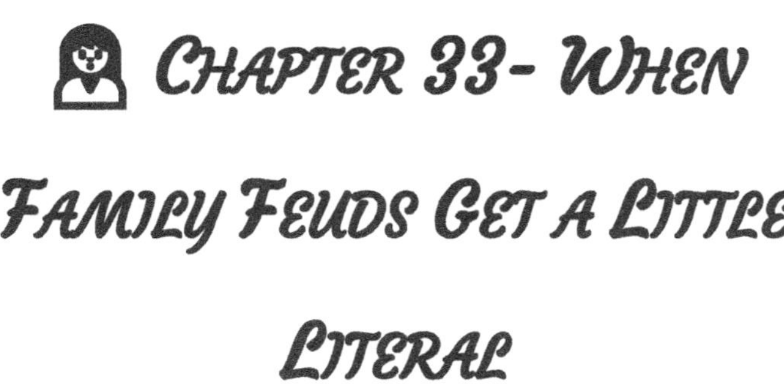 Chapter 33- When Family Feuds Get a Little Literal

Chapter 33- When Family Feuds Get a Little Literal

"Mom?" My mother smiled, happy to be recognized. "Calliope," she said, her tone serious, "I need you to take your friends out of here." I stood up and pushed away a flabbergasted Hades. "No," I answered my mother like the impromptu, reckless, disobedient girl I am. "I am not leaving you when you need us most, Mom," I continued, notching an arrow and aiming at Hades' face. I expected to get scolded, but instead, I got a warm smile from my mom. "That's my incautious daughter," she said, drawing a crystalline knife. The splotches of dried blood told me that this was something my mother used often. "Mrs. Canderine!" shouted Kay, who, while fighting, had just realized that my mom was here. "Hello to you, too, McKayla," she answered. "Let's turn this tide!" my mother yelled, thrusting her hands upwards. I stared as the skeletons that were once fighting my friends and obeying Hades, were now attacking their previous master. "You shall serve me!" Mom yelled, pointing at the skeleton guards and commanding them to charge at her father. I stared in awe. "Why haven't I seen you do this before?" I asked my mother, with beads forming on her forehead. "I didn't want to scare you, Calli." "And also, when did you find out about our idea?" I asked.

"Not telling you," she answered sternly. "I need to know!" I yelled back. "Did Ra- I mean Ms. A tell you?" She shook her head. "Why were you going to say your teacher's first name?" "Because she made us call her Raya," I replied matter-of-factly, as if my mom wasn't currently leading an assault against her father and my grandfather. "GAAAAHH!" he yelled, attacking his former guards with his light. Suddenly, my mother faltered and lost control of the guards, who ran towards my friends. "Mom!" I yelled, frantically finding some ambrosia. I did find some, so I gave it to my mother, who looked deathly pale. "Go help your friends, Calli," she said weakly. "But-" "They need you. GO!"

I ran towards Kay, who was desperately trying to find more pouches with seeds on her belt. "Incoming!" I yelled and, with a little concentration, dark light shot through my palm and disintegrated about 3 skeletons. "Calli!" Kay exclaimed, wrapping me in a hug and swinging me around wildly. (which, taking in the fact that she was 5' 1" and I was 5' 4", I didn't think she was capable of). "Stop hugging and fight!" Chris screamed, his eyes fierce, running another sword through a guard's gut. I turned around and found a skeleton about to shoot me with a rifle. I quickly drew an arrow and shot him instead. I turned to Chris and smiled annoyingly. "I guess I can do both at the same time." He rolled his eyes, but he couldn't hide the wide smile on his face.

My heart fluttered inside my chest. You are not helping! I told my heart, which didn't stop. So inconsiderate. "FATHER!" my mom's voice echoed through the throne room. We all stopped, momentarily. Even the skeletons. "That is enough! You have taken this too far!" she yelled. "We both know this isn't what we had agreed on!" Agreed on? My mother had an agreement with Hades, the guy who was trying to kill me. Hades put on a smug smile, and walked towards

my mother. "Perhaps you are right, Cyrene."
"Guards!" All the skeletons turned towards their master. "Positions!" Positions?

All the guards walked to where they were when we first arrived. "Calli?" Chris asked on my left. "I have no idea what in the world is happening right now," I answered his silent question. "Mom? What is this?" I asked her, my eyes full of concern. She smiled and slightly inclined her head to Hades, whose smug smile now showed something other than hatred. I had seen that smile before, in the mirror after awards ceremonies and compliments. Pride. "Calliope Canderine," he called out. I raised an eyebrow, unsure of what to do. "Come here, Granddaughter." I snorted. "So you can, what, try to kill me again?" His smile suddenly looked strained. "Just listen to me so that won't happen again." "Father!" my mom reminded him.

"Excuse me," he said in return, gesturing to come to him. I took my time to limp over there. Hey, I was being called by the same dude who hurt my foot, took my mother's magic, and practically ruined my life. It was now my mother's turn to show pride. Later, my friends told me that while I stood next to Hades, my eyes showed confusion mixed with rage. Do you blame me, though? "Calliope Canderine," Hades repeated my name. "You have exceeded all our expectations in the best way possible, by completing this quest."

"What expectations?" I asked, being the blabbermouth I am. My mother laughed gently and looked me in the eyes. She lifted her palm, and a small purple tornado thingy appeared on it. "Your magic," I realized, "It's back."

"How could it be back?" she answered, "When it was never away." My eyes widened with surprise. I quickly stepped away from my mother and grandfather, walked to my friends, put on a serious face, and crossed my arms across my chest. "I need an explanation. Right. Now."

Chapter 34- Hades, Mom, and a Quest Gone Awry

Chapter 34- Hades, Mom, and a Quest Gone Awry

My expression was supposed to make my mom and Hades cower in fear. Instead, they laughed at me. Yes, dear reader. You heard me right. The God of the Dead and my mother, the ferocious sorcerous, were laughing at me as if what I was doing was naive. Now that I think back, it probably was. My mother walked towards me with a gentle smile on her face, a smile I haven't seen since I was 8. "Let me explain." "See, when you were upstairs working on that photography project, which I hope is now completed, I told my father, Hades, that you were ready for your first quest. Hades wasn't so sure, but I knew that whatever you had faced, it was all put in your journey to make you the amazing girl you are now. Anyways, I knew that you hated my sorcery, it's okay, your dad wasn't very fond of it either, but I knew, deep down, that you would do anything to keep me safe and happy, yes?" I nodded. Since when did my mother start lecturing me about the 'amazing girl' I am. She continued. "So, if we were successful in calling Hades, even though we were finding Oliver, Hades could pretend to take away my magic, making me upset. And if I am upset, and don't you deny it, Calli, you get upset, too. After the entire 'meeting godly grandfather' and 'having magic taken away', I knew you would find the books we bought for you in Greece. The ones about the myths. You would try to find out more about Hades and this world, and you would decide to come here, to the Underworld, and convince him to get my magic back. And, McKayla being your best friend, and also the only one who knew about my magic, you would talk her into coming with you. And that worked," she stopped to take a breath. I stared at her with wide eyes. She knew practically the entire game plan, the plan which I thought I was hiding from her. She continued. "But, I didn't know that Chris would come into account as well. Still, he did, and here he is now. Anyways, I knew something would happen at school as well, like developing new powers and things like that. I found out that you discovered your power because of that girl, Carissa. And, that Ms. Arnyam had caught y'all and told you about her relation to Lethe and Hecate. Raya and I used to be neighbors; that's why she knew about Hades being my father. Raya had conferred with me about what you kids were doing and how strong Calli was. And, I also knew about your plan to go to Space Center Houston, the entrance to Hades. When Ms. Arnyam had dropped you off at the training center, she had come immediately to pick me up, and she also dropped me here. Since I was Hades' daughter, I got privileges. By privileges, I mean I could command any creature in the Underworld who obeyed my father, and they would have to comply. So, I commanded the Furies to bring me here. And here I am," she finished. I was stunned. "So, you knew this whole time?" I asked. My mom smiled. "Of course I did." My friends and I had overlooked the fact that my mom could've been in cahoots with Hades. "Personally," Chris said, "Your mom's cool. I mean, anybody who can figure out our plan without us telling them has to be cool, right?"

My mom laughed. "I will take that as a compliment, Chris. Thank you." "So," Kay said, "Are we going to go home now?" But right after she said it, she staggered forward. She would have bitten grass if Chris and I hadn't caught her. Her head lolled. "Kay!" I yelled. There was no answer.

Chapter 35- I Have an Emotional Breakdown

Chapter 35- I Have an Emotional Breakdown

"Mom! Help!" I yelled across the room. My mother understood. She quickly came over and picked up an unconscious McKayla, while Hades, surprisingly, teleported us to Persephone's garden. We laid her down on a flat rock, but Kay hadn't opened her eyes yet. She was still breathing, thankfully. I couldn't restrain the tears falling down my face. I mean, would you not do the same? "Kay," I said between sobs, "Wake up." I turned to my mom and Hades. "Do something!" I met Hades' gaze. "Aren't you a god or something? Help her!" He shook his head.

"Even I cannot do anything, unfortunately." I pulled out some Ambrosia and nectar, and force-fed Kay. "We need to take her outside of the Underworld," I told Hades firmly. He cocked an eyebrow. "And why can we not stay here?" "She is a legacy of Demeter, her granddaughter. I am pretty sure this place has been draining her energy since we've arrived. Remember, Chris, when she fell when we were walking in the tunnel which led to here?" He nodded. "Yeah. I think taking her to the upper world, to the sun and nature, would probably help her." Hades nodded. "Wait," said a voice behind us. It was Persephone.

"We are in a garden, surrounded by nature," she said, waving at her garden. "This cannot be enough?" I shook my head. "Unless you guys have some healing abilities..." I glanced at Hades. "Other than the God of the Dead, I mean." He glared at me, but I glared back. I wasn't scared of him anymore. But when was I even scared? "Fine," Hades grumbled and snapped his fingers. Don't worry, Kay, I thought, we will save you.

🤣 Chapter 36- The Giver Makes a Come- Back

Chapter 36- The Giver Makes a Come- Back

We appeared outside of the Underworld, finally. The warmth of the Sun was a change from the cold and damp environment of Hades. We were in a field with cows around us. The field looked distantly familiar, though I couldn't place where I last saw it. "Where are we?" I asked. "I am guessing this is Space Center Houston," my mother replied. I turned towards Kay, who was in my mother's arms, her eyes still shut. My eyes stung. I couldn't help but still feel guilty. She came to the Underworld because of me. She felt unconscious multiple times during this trip because of me. She was kidnapped by the Furies because of me. Kay stayed back to fight the guards of Hades because of me. And now, she is in some kind of coma after taxing her energy a lot because of me. What kind of friend am I? "Hey," said a voice behind me. It was Chris putting his hand on my shoulder. "She'll be fine, you know?"

I nodded as tears fell down my face. He quickly enveloped me in his strong arms, my face buried in his shoulder as I cried. I could feel my mom staring at us, but I didn't care. I pretended that everything was alright, even though I knew it wasn't. I just needed somebody to comfort me, you know?

I pulled away, sniffling and wiping tears. "Thanks. I needed that, Clown," I said, adding a smile at the last word. Chris smiled back. "I'll always give you what you need, Captain." I laughed. But a thought jarred me like lightning. Kay. I forgot about her.

I looked back at my unconscious friend, then back at Chris. "Let's take her to a hospital."

He raised an eyebrow. "We have no other option, Chris! She may be dead or dying, and she is just... there. Lying down in the Sun, like it has some healing powers or something!" He nodded and pulled out his olive-green phone. There was something new on the phone. The cover had splotches of grey, the same shade that my eyes are.

I ignored that fact as Chris opened Google Maps and found that the nearest hospital was about 15 minutes away.

I faced Kay, who was being bandaged by my mother. McKayla had little cuts and scratches on her arms, her legs (cut through her jeans overalls), and even on her face. "Good afternoon, darlings. May I be of assistance?" Chris jumped in shock as I turned around. To my surprise, it was Hermes, willing to help us.

"Dude," Chris said, "Don't do that! You almost gave me a heart attack!" Hermes slightly tilted his head. "Did I? I am sorry." I blinked. A god saying sorry? I could also get used to this. "I will repeat my question," he said calmly. "May I be of any assistance?"

I look towards Kay, laying down with her eyes closed.

I take a deep breath. "Yes, Lord Hermes. Please." He cocked an eyebrow. "How may I help?"

I pointed to McKayla. "My friend taxed too much of her energy in the Underworld, and now she is unconscious. She can't seem to wake up, even after multiple doses of Ambrosia and

Nectar. He nodded. "I see. I believe you will have some luck with the mortal hospitals. Even finding Apollo, the god of healing, or

Asclepius, the god of doctors. I could help you find them, if you want."

I brought my 'sweet girl' voice and said, "Thank you, Lord Hermes. Please help us save McKayla." Hermes grinned. Then, he spotted Hades and Persephone. "Uncle! Sister! I didn't see you there!" he called out, and the gods just turned around with annoyance on their faces. "Hello, Hermes," Hades said, as if he just realized his nephew was there. "I am going to take the mortals to Apollo and Asclepius, so you may go back to your palace," Hades grunted. "Come on, my love," he said to Persephone, who nodded. Soon, my grandfather and his wife disappeared into the shadows.

I walked towards Kay. "We will save you, Kay. Just... hang on, alright." No answer.

My mom, who was tending to McKayla's wounds, rubbed my back. I nodded and quickly pulled away, determined not to show my weak side. My mom picked up Kay and walked towards Hermes and Chris, who wrapped his arm around me. Mom raised an eyebrow, but I pretended I didn't see. "Are you ready?" the god of travelers asked. We nodded. "Here we go, then. We are going to find my brother Apollo and his son Asclepius at the hospital nearby." We just nodded, not knowing what else to do. Soon, everything went black.

Chapter 37- We Go See Godly Physicians

Chapter 37- We Go See Godly Physicians

When we came to, we found ourselves in a brightly lit hospital room, with 2 young men wearing lab coats. The first one had long, golden hair, which was tied up. He was beardless, but his face was too perfect for him to be human. His eyes were the color of gold, and it was too bright to look at. The other man looked younger, if anything. He had a short beard and long hair (also tied back), though. In his hand was a staff with 1 snake curled around it (unlike Hermes', who had 2). I bowed. "Lord Apollo and Lord Asclepius." The one with the staff was Asculepius, and the one with the golden eyes was his father, Apollo.

Asclepius smiled. "I am glad to be recognized." "You must be Calliope Canderine, granddaughter of Hades, yes?" Apollo asked. I nodded. "Yes, sir. And we have a request for you." I waved to my mother, who was still carrying Kay. She walked forwards and laid McKayla down on the bed. "This is my best friend, McKayla Carson, granddaughter of Demeter," I explained. "While in the Underworld on a quest, which went wrong, all her energy was depleted after fighting and staying without the Sun for so long. Now, she is unconscious and not even Nectar and Ambrosia can wake her up. Lord Hermes," I turned to find him, but he was nowhere to be seen. "I mean, he told us that you two can help us. So, please, can you fix her?" I asked with a hopeful tone added to my 'sweet girl' voice.

(I learned that when I channel it, I get more things done, especially with gods.) Apollo turned to his son. "Asclepius, this is far from my skills. You can help them, but I cannot. My powers won't be of any help, here." The god of doctors nodded. "I understand, Father." Apollo turned to me. "My son will help your friend. And," he said, "I shall be off. I promised the Muses that I will come join their concert today on Mount Olympus." I bowed again. "Thank you, Apollo and Asclepius." I looked up, and found that the god of prophecy was gone. He was going to a concert with my namesake and her sisters. Ugh. I would pick a concert over what was happening right now. Asclepius closed his eyes in concentration. So did I, thinking that I might lend some of my energy to him and Kay. A breeze whipped my hair on my face. Ouch. I felt somebody holding my hand. Chris, I thought. Either he was scared, or he just wanted to hold my hand. (Both of them felt appropriate at the time. If he did that now, I would tease Hades out of him.) Suddenly, the wind stopped. I opened my eyes. Kay was still lying there with her eyes closed, the only movement she was making was the rise and fall of her chest. I crossed my fingers and shut my eyes tightly. I couldn't stand anything happening to her. I kept on praying to anybody who would listen; that was how desperate I was. I cracked open my eyes and saw McKayla. Her eyes were open, showing her beautiful hazel irises. My own eyes widened as I yelled her name.

☺ Chapter 38- Kay Wakes Up

Chapter 38- Kay Wakes Up & Immediately Tries to Get Me Killed

"MCKAYLA!" I yelled as tears streamed down my face. She slowly sat up, smirking. "Hello to you too, Ca-" I interrupted her with a huge hug, crying into her shoulder. "Calm down, Calli," Kay said, taking me back to my dad's funeral. "It'll be alright." I kept on sobbing. I was crying so much that it took both my mom and Chris to pull me away. "Gosh, Calli," McKayla said with a smile. "I haven't seen you cry this much since we were 8." I rolled my eyes. Between sniffles, I thanked Asclepius, who was standing in a corner, grinning at the scene. He smiled at my thanks, and teleported away to who- knows- where. "Kay," I said, "I thought you were dead." "You didn't think that I would die in such an extravagant way, did you?" I laughed half-heartedly. My mom decided that she and Chris should leave Kay and me alone, so they left the room. "I would never forgive myself if my best friend, come sister, had died because of me. I mean, I was the one who told you to come along. And I was the one who made you faint in the cavern. And I was the one who you stayed back and fought for. So, in short, if you had died, it would be because of me." Kay laughed at me. Yes, my friend, you read that right. I poured my freaking heart out, and she LAUGHED at me! If this were back at home, I would beat her up (no guarantee if I would actually or not), but in those circumstances, I just gave her the death stare, which cracked her up even more. "Dude," she said in between giggles, "I'm stronger than you think. Also, if I had, you know, died, it would be because of that creep,

Hades." "I agree with the fact that he is a creep, alongside my grandfather." Then, I stage-whispered, "Who don't I really like that much?" She laughed again. Ugh, stop laughing! I was being legitimately serious. Once she stopped giggling, she said, "So, what's up with you and Chris?" I blushed. "Um..." "What happened after I was kidnapped by Hades?" I found a sudden interest in my flower-patterned Converse. Kay started grinning. "Did y'all hugged?"

I'm pretty sure my face turned, like, three more shades of darker red. "I think, like, twice?" This made her laugh. Again. God, did Asclepius' healing have any side effects, like laughing at everything, etc? "OMG! I totally shipped y'all since, like, I first saw you two walking down the hall with each other!" she said, ending her sentence with a squeal. "Bro,

I don't even think we are in a relationship. More like a situationship." "STILL! Oh my gosh, what did your mom say?" "She saw us hugging, it was when you were still unconscious. She didn't say anything, but she stared at us and raised multiple eyebrows," I mumbled. "AAAHH!! I am SO HAPPY!" she said, trying to dance while sitting up on a hospital bed.

"Why are you so happy?" I asked with annoyance. "BECAUSE, firstly, my 2 best friends, whom I shipped 24/7, are now together, and secondly, MY OTP IS CANON!!!" I blinked multiple times. "They're practically the same thing." "IT DOESN'T MATTER!" I rolled my eyes. "But," she said with a smirk. "I am going to be the bride's maid and/ or the flower girl at y'all's wedding, right?" I slapped her hand, my face now tomato red. "SHUT UP OR YOU WILL WISH

YOU WERE DEAD!!!" Kay kept on smirking. Save me from this lunatic. Chris thought this was the right time to knock on the door and enter the room. I was blushing furiously, and McKayla was laughing like crazy.

"Um," he said with an uncertain expression, "Did I miss something important?" Before I could tell Kay to shut up, she said, "Oh, it's nothing. I was just talking about shipping you and Calli. But, you may leave the room, if you want." He stared at me and I rolled my eyes in annoyance. Goodness, I was just crying for the girl, and now the girl in question was trying to kill me. What type of bestie does that? We walked over to me, my face, like, crimson red. "Now that I think of it," he said nonchalantly, taking my hand, "I think I ship us too." I didn't think I could blush even harder, but, to my surprise, I did. "Do you, Captain?" he asked, squeezing my hand. I barely nodded.

"I might not know what 'shipping' is, but if it's about Calli and Chris, I might 'ship' you both, too," said my mom. I actually got jump-scared, cracking up both Kay and Chris. I hoped that that laughing virus wasn't coming towards me. "So," I asked uncertainly, "You aren't going to say no?" "Why would I?" she countered. "I mean, I met your father the same age that you are. And, you two are horribly cute together. Horrible, meaning that if you aren't with each other, it will be horrible for me." I blinked, again, multiple times. Who is this, and where is my sorceress of a mother? "Now," I said, clearing my throat. "How do we get out of here?" "Leave it to me," my mom said with a grin which made me glad that she was on my side. Soon, we were surrounded by shadows.

🏠 *Chapter 39*- Home Swee-

OMG

Chapter 39- Home Swee- OMG! WHO IS THAT!

We reappeared at my house, specifically, in the living room. I whooped loudly, pumping my fists into the air. I was home! Kay staggered forward, but didn't fall this time (courtesy of my mother dear). I hugged McKayla, who complained about her ribs being broken (spoiler alert: they weren't, and if they were, I didn't care). Then, I hugged my mom, letting go of all the resentment I had ever felt for her, and letting in all the love I had for her. She smelled like cinnamon, not my favorite smell, but it smelled like home. Before I could react, Chris picked me up and spun me around wildly. I guess I forgot to tell him I had tachophobia (the fear of speed). Then, he put me down and gave me a bear hug, which I returned. Right when we pulled away, I went on my tippy-toes, and gave him a quick hug, my heart racing. Then, Kay started whooping. "MY OTP IS REAL! OMG! OMG! AAHHHH!" Mom had to calm her down, but she gave me a small smile, like she was happy, for once. I felt happy, myself. But Hades wasn't over yet. My godly grandfather appeared in front of our joyous group. My mother was the first one to recover. "Father," she said sternly, "What are you here for?" He smiled. "Why, I haven't given Calliope her reward yet!" "M-my reward?" I asked skeptically. "I think you will like it."

He looked back, and suddenly, I saw a ghost. The spirit had retro glasses, pitch black eyes, and a smile which was nothing like his eyes. I teared up. My mother realized who it was at the same time I did. "Dad?" The spirit nodded.

Chapter 40 – My Mother Succeeds on Her Mission

Chapter 40- My Mother Succeeds on her Mission

"Oliver?" my mom asked the spirit in front of us. "Cyrene," he said with a smile. My mom fell to her knees with broken sobs. I didn't do any better. "My muse," he called, "Come here." "D- dad!" I yelled, running towards him. I expected to pass right through him, since he was a ghost, but his solid arms wrapped around me as I sobbed into his chest. He slowly caressed my dirty-blonde hair, muttering endearing words. "Mr. Canderine!" Kay said with a smile, and tears welled up in her eyes. "Hello, McKayla," he said with a grin. Then, he looked down at the crying me. "You have grown so much, My Muse," he said. "And I am so proud of you."

"And you guys, too, Kay and Chris," he said to my friends. "How do you know my name?" Chris asked, bewildered. "I like to keep myself posted." My mom got up and ran to my dad. He wrapped her in a hug, too. "I miss you, Oliver, so much," she said between sniffles. "And me too, Cyrene. I miss both of you," he said, causing me to cry harder. "And, I see that you listened to me, my love," he said. My mom nodded. "It was hard convincing my father, but she passed." Passed? She? Convincing Hades? They all added up to one thing, resulting in me having a flashback. My dad had whispered something in my mom's ear before the launch. "Dad?" I asked quietly. "Yes, my muse?"

"Did you tell Mom that she should test me on a quest when I was 12?" I asked. He gently kissed the top of my head. "I'm surprised you saw me whisper that in your mom's ear." "It took me a while, but I realized soon enough." He chuckled. "You are your mother's daughter." My mom pulled away from my dad with tears in her eyes. She turned to her father. "I thought you didn't like bringing the dead to the normal world," she said, her voice cracking on 'dead'. Hades smiled. (If you didn't know, Hades' smile looks pretty smug.) "I guess I made an exception for you both." Then, he faced Chris. "Oh, I forgot another soul. One moment." Soon, Chris was facing a tall woman with dark, curly hair and chocolate eyes.

"My little boy," said the woman with a smile. I had seen that woman before, on Chris' phone. It was his mom. "M- mom?" he asked skeptically, walking towards her and giving her his signature bear hug. The woman laughed in a sophisticated manner. "You are so big now, Chris." Chris had tears in his eyes. He nodded. Then, he turned to Hades. "Thank you," he said. I turned to my dad. "You have to go soon, don't you?" He sadly nodded. "Alas, I am not really alive right now, am I? And I must return to the Underworld, my Muse." I ran to Hades and gave him a huge hug. He was stunned, and his face was, according to my friends, priceless. "Thanks, Grandfather," I said.

He only nodded his head and quickly pulled away. Kay was talking to my dad right after, probably catching him up on everything. Even me and Chris. My dad looked at me and smiled. "You are definitely not the little girl who I left behind. Physically, emotionally, and mentally." I dipped my head a little. Nah, really? The annoying part of me said in my head. "Calliope, Chris, McKayla," Hades said. "It is time for them to go." My eyes widened. No, no, I wasn't ready to lose Dad again. I went to him and gave him another hug, which he quickly melted into. "Don't worry," he whispered in my ear. "I will be back one time or another." That was my dad; always trying to be positive, even if the situation was negative two billion.

I pulled away, wiping my tears. My mom was the opposite. I mean, she couldn't pull away; that was how hard she was crying. "Shh," my dad said. "Like I told Calli, I will come back. Just like the stars, the moon, and the Sun do." Another one of my dad's traits: he will find a way to bring the Universe into every conversation. My mom laughed half-heartedly and, surprisingly, pulled away. Chris was just finishing his goodbyes with his mom. We walked towards me, and the two ghosts went towards my grandad. Hades gave us a little wave, and in the blink of an eye, all three of them were gone.

⌷ᴼˢ CHAPTER 41- KAY FANGIRLS OVER US... SEND HELP

Chapter 41- Kay Fangirls Over Us... Send Help

It had been 2 weeks since we finished our quest. I was with my best friends (one of them with whom I was in a situationship) and we were sitting at the cafeteria table on the last day of school. We just came from photography (Kay had asked for a schedule change, and, surprisingly, she got theater as well as photography. Ms. Arnyam was still the best, in case you were wondering.) It was just the three of us, since our 'normal friends' decided they didn't like us, and thought that we brought a 'weird vibe to the table'. If only they knew... We were talking about our grades on the previous math test (which Chris definitely failed) when they called our table for lunch. Kay was the only one from our part of the row who went to get her lunch, since Chris and I both brought our meals. Needless to say, it was kind of awkward between us two. In the past, we had shared multiple hugs, a couple of hold-hands, and infinite life- or- death situations. Slowly, Chris brought out a little baggie from his backpack. It had glitter and all that stuff on it. Inside, there was a dark purple bead bracelet. I realized, suddenly, that Chris wore that same bracelet to school today. He blushed. "Um.. so, I thought you might like this, and it might, you know, officialize us, you know, like us us... like a-- "Shut up for a minute," I told him, and he obliged. "You are soooo adorable, Clown. The color is pretty, you know? I will take it, and I understand what you mean by us, you ding-dong. I didn't fail that math test, you know?" He glared at me, and I glared back. "You get so annoying, Captain." "And you too, Clown."

"But, you sure you want the bracelet?" "Yes," I said firmly, "And the officializing of, you know…" "Yeah," he said with a smirk, "I know." He handed the baggie and I took out the beautiful bracelet.

It fit perfectly on my wrist. "Thank you, Chris." "You are welcome, Calli."

I laughed. "Since when are we so formal with each other?" He started grinning. "I blame you." That was right when Kay decided to come and sit next to me. "Guys," she said, "Do I feel a development in Camperine?" "What?" Chris and I said in sync. "Y'all even say the same thing at the same time, that's adorbs. I mean, that's y'all's ship name. Campbell and Canderine make Camperine." We stared at her with annoyance.

"I tried adding y'all's first name, but Chrisiope just sounds weird."

I laughed. "Nooo, that is the best name in the world." We all started cracking up.

I met Chris' gaze. He grinned. "Yeah," he said, reaching out for my hand," there is a development." McKayla started whopping so loud that the assistant principal, Ms. Hail, came over and gave us a warning. That just made us laugh even harder. Fast forward to the end of the day. We were going to walk home that day, since our bus broke down on the way. We brought Kay up to speed on what happened when she went to get lunch. She started giggling. "You two are never gonna get any less cuter!" she squealed. "Shut up, Kay," I grumbled, but deep down, I was really happy. I had an amazing best friend and a trustworthy boyfriend. My mother went back to magic, and

I was delighted to help her. So were Chris and Kay. We were just about to enter our street when we saw a familiar figure at the pole. "Guys," I said, tentatively, "Do you see that person there?" They nodded. The figure turned to us and grinned widely. "Hello, darlings!" waved the messenger god Hermes. We walked towards him. "Hello, Hermes," Kay said. "What do you want?"

I didn't blame her for being so rude to Hermes. I would've done that too if she hadn't opened her mouth first. I mean, yes, he did help us, but we were kind of annoyed from the quest-thingy we had to go on for no reason, you know?

"Oh, dear," he said. "You three look unpleasant. If I were in your place, I would too." "To rephrase McKayla's question," I said. "What are you here for?" "Why, to ask for a favor!" Chris groaned. "Dude. We literally just came back from a mission, and you want us to go on another one??" Yep. We were pretty annoyed. "I want you to help greet my grandchildren who will be moving to your school next year. It is the last day before summer, yes?" We nodded. "Who are your grandchildren?" I asked. "Oh, their names are Naina and Aisha Chatti, ages 14 and 12." "Naina will be in your grade, while Aisha will just start middle school. They will be there on the first day, so beware!"

Hermes vanished in a puff of smoke. I turned to my friends. "Looks like we just got ourselves another mission."

😃 Heroes and their Appearance

Heroes and Their Appearance (by order of appearance)

1. *CALLIOPE CANDERINE-*

   a. Age- 12

   b. Eye color- stormy grey

   c. Hair color- dirty blonde

   d. Hair type- straight w/ curls at the end

   e. Height- 5'4" Skin color- light tan

   f. Fav color- Magenta, she can't pick between pink and purple

   g. Fav food- Dragon fruit

   h. Extra- Lost father age 8, loves photography, *** spoilers ***, very loyal, Grandaughter of Hades, mother does sorcery

2. *CHRIS CAMPBELL*-

    a. Age- 12

    b. Eye color- dark chocolate brown

    c. Hair- black, curly hair

    d. Height- 5'6"

    e. Skin color- sandy

    f. Fav color- Green, like his mom's eyes and dark grey, like Calli's eyes

    g. Fav food- Mint cookies, which he was eating in the car on the way to Space Center Houston Extra-Grandson of Aphrodite, ********* spoilers******, (pretty eyes according to Calli)

3. *McKAYLA CARSON*-

    a. Age- 13

    b. Eye color- hazel

c. Hair color- brown

d. Hair type- curly and luxurious

e. Height- 5'1"

f. Skin color- beige

g. Fav color- Maroon

h. Fav food- Chocolate chip muffins, the ones her mom makes

i. Extra- wears maroon colored glasses, not very smart, *******Spoilers*********, in theater (amazing actress according to Calli)

4. **Ms. Arnyam or Raya**

a. Age- 33

b. Eye color- light grey

c. Hair color- blackish- brown

d. Hair type- silky

e. Height- 5' 7"

f. Skin color- light brown

g. Fav color- Silver grey, like her favorite camera

h. Fav food- Donuts, has donut themed things on her desk

i. Extra- Photography teacher at Paideia Middle School, Daughter of Hecate and granddaughter of Lethe

ACKNOWLEDGMENTS-

Acknowledgments-

Just so y'all know, it took me a really long time to decide how to write this. Honestly. You can ask my mom or my brother anytime. Anyways, I think I'm going to have to thank my mother. A lot. She always urged me to write, and, me being a stubborn child, I hated writing back then. If only the past Samara met the Samara I am now... Goodness, I am getting seriously off track. So, as I was saying, through my months of craziness and ranting about Calliope and her friends, my mother would listen calmly and give me advice. She came from a family in literature, so she was one of the best people to help me. My dad also listened while I talked about The Dark Curse, and there is a part of him in Oliver Canderine which my subconscious decided to align.

I am going to regret this, but I must thank my younger brother, Taha. Even though he is the uttermost annoying person I have ever met, when nobody listened to me, he did and still does. And I am really thankful for the support. (He better be really grateful that I said that...) Oh! I cannot miss my 7th-grade language arts teacher, Mrs. Craig. The Dark Curse actually started out as a short story Mrs. Craig gave out in class on Halloween. And, she also gave me a bunch of suggestions while writing, so I am truly grateful. One last person whom I really need to thank is one of my good friends, Anyela. She was writing her own book when I wrote this, so we both were each other's emotional support. Like, when she read chapter 11, she was like, "Gurl, what do you mean that happened to her!!!" And I was like, "Thank my hyperfixations for that..." Speaking of hyperfixations, I have to thank all the books in my room (and in the bookshelf in the game room). As a bookworm, (people at my school call me that and I will never deny it.) I need my books, the characters in them, the adventures they go through, to realize, woah. My life can either suck like that, or stay the same way. Sometimes, though, I can't pick... ANYWAYS, I couldn't have survived this process without them, so thank you for keeping me sane and alive :)

THE
DARK
CURSE

In a world where ancient myths whisper secrets to the living, twelve-year-old Calliope Canderine thought her biggest worry was finishing her photography collage. But when a botched spell summons her godly grandfather, none other than Hades himself, her life spirals into chaos. Stripped of her sorcery powers, Calli's mom is left heartbroken, and Calli? She's furious. Determined to set things right, she hatches a daring plan: venture into the shadowy depths of the Underworld to confront the God of the Dead and demand her family's magic back.

Joined by her quick-witted best friend McKayla and the charming new kid Chris (who harbors his own divine secrets), Calli embarks on a whirlwind quest filled with alligator nightmares, shadowy powers awakening within her, and encounters with gods who'd rather forget mortals exist. From the bustling halls of Paideia Middle School to the eerie gates of Hades' palace, they'll dodge Furies, unravel family curses, and face heart-wrenching flashbacks that blur the line between past traumas and present perils.

But as alliances shift and hidden truths emerge, Calli must question: Is this curse a punishment... or a path to discovering her true strength?

Brimming with Greek mythology twists, heartfelt friendships, and pulse-pounding adventure, The Dark Curse is a spellbinding tale of loss, legacy, and the magic that binds us. Perfect for fans of Percy Jackson who crave a fresh heroine's voice.

BY SAMARA HUSSAIN